MEET T̶̶̶̶̶̶̶̶̶̶

Fortune of the Month: Delaney Fortune Jones

Age: 24

Vital statistics: A petite and perky spitfire. You'll never see her without her cowboy boots.

Claim to Fame: The youngest of Jeanne Marie Fortune Jones's children, Delaney always calls 'em as she sees 'em.

Romantic prospects: She is currently being courted by Miami native Cisco Mendoza. But she is doing her best to resist...

"Maybe every girl in town has had her head turned by Cisco Mendoza. But I refuse to be swayed by his city-slicker swagger and his sophisticated ways. I'm in search of a solid cowboy, not a tourist. So what if he makes my stomach do a two-step? I'm *not* going to be roped in by chocolate-brown eyes and sweet nothings. But what if...*what if* I could wrangle Cisco's heart for real?"

THE FORTUNES OF TEXAS: COWBOY COUNTRY—
Lassoing hearts from across the pond!

Dear Reader,

What a thrill to be part of the Fortunes of Texas continuity. I loved discovering more about the town of Horseback Hollow and wish I could spend a day at Deke and Jeanne Marie's ranch!

Delaney Fortune Jones is one of my favorite heroines, spunky and sure of herself. She knows exactly who she is in life, a true American girl. As for what she wants, Delaney thinks she has that figured out as well—until she meets Cisco Mendoza.

For Cisco, success is a given, and he's in Horseback Hollow to close the biggest deal of his career. The only catch is he needs a Fortune to make it happen. It doesn't seem difficult—and then Delaney changes everything. This cowgirl and her city slicker have a lot to learn about each other and what it takes to find a happy-ever-after. I hope you enjoy their journey to love as much as I did.

I'd love to hear more about your favorite Fortunes. Drop me an email at michelle@michellemajor.com.

Happy reading!

Michelle Major

The Taming of
Delaney Fortune

—

Michelle Major

HARLEQUIN®SPECIAL EDITION®

Special thanks and acknowledgment to Michelle Major for her contribution to the Fortunes of Texas: Cowboy Country continuity.

Recycling programs
for this product may
not exist in your area.

ISBN-13: 978-0-373-65877-0

The Taming of Delaney Fortune

Copyright © 2015 by Harlequin Books S.A.

This edition published by arrangement with Harlequin Books S.A.

For questions and comments about the quality of this book, please contact us at CustomerService@Harlequin.com.

Printed in U.S.A.

www.Harlequin.com

Michelle Major grew up in Ohio but dreamed of living in the mountains. Soon after graduating with a degree in journalism, she pointed her car west and settled in Colorado. Her life and house are filled with one great husband, two beautiful kids, a few furry pets and several well-behaved reptiles. She's grateful to have found her passion writing stories with happy endings. Michelle loves to hear from her readers at michellemajor.com.

Books by Michelle Major

Harlequin Special Edition

Visit the Author Profile page at Harlequin.com for more titles.

To the Fortunes of Texas: Cowboy Country team—
Susan and Marcia, Judy, Cindy, Marie, Nancy
and Allison. Thanks for being so welcoming!

Prologue

Delaney Fortune Jones was a romantic at heart. She loved Valentine's Day as much as she loved weddings. But it took a bit of work to convince herself that the tears she'd shed today, watching four of her siblings get married, were only the joyful kind.

Of course she was happy for Jude, Liam, Christopher and Stacey. They'd each found the love of their lives, and Delaney had been thrilled and honored to stand up as a bridesmaid while they said their vows. The ceremony had taken place earlier on the beautiful Parthenon-inspired stage that had been built next to the barn on her parents' ranch. Each couple's vows had been personal to their relationship, but when the ball of emotion wedged in Delaney's throat as she listened, there was a wistful edge to it.

Only she and her brother Galen were single now. Delaney would be the last of Deke and Jeanne Marie's children still living on the ranch after today. Her world had shifted, and she knew it would never be the same.

But Delaney was a romantic and an optimist. She believed she'd find true love someday. It was only a matter of time until the right cowboy came along to share the small-town life she treasured. Horseback Hollow, Texas, wasn't big or fancy, but it was the only home she'd ever need.

Shaking her head, she took a breath and then a deeper breath. Her parents had transformed the barn for the reception, but underneath the flowers and candles, Delaney could still smell the comforting scent of hay and horses. The barn was her happy place, and looking around at all of the people she loved gathered together tonight chased away her brooding thoughts.

She tapped her cowboy boot along with the rhythm to a popular song, watching her family and friends on the dance floor. She'd changed from heels after the ceremony, but the pink shell inlay of the boots still matched her silk bridesmaid's gown. Her young nieces and nephews ran around the edge of the dance floor, stopping to wiggle their hips as the tempo increased. Delaney laughed out loud but didn't move to join them. She was good at a lot of things. Dancing wasn't one of them.

However, the bar was set up on the far side of the barn, so she made her way through the crowd as the music ended. A woman turned as Delaney went to slide past her, and Delaney blinked several times. Shannon Singleton, who Delaney had known since they were girls, looked stunning in her black lace dress. The light in her eyes made her even more gorgeous.

"Delaney," Shannon said as she gave her a quick hug, "Wasn't it a beautiful ceremony?"

"The most beautiful," Delaney agreed, but Shannon had already turned away, pulling a man forward.

"Delaney, have you met Cisco Mendoza?" Shannon asked. "He's one of Gabi's handsome brothers."

"The most handsome," the man murmured with a deep chuckle.

"Absolutely," Shannon agreed with a bright laugh. "But don't tell the rest of them I said so. Cisco, this is Delaney Fortune, the baby of the family."

"Not quite a baby," Delaney muttered, feeling her cheeks flame.

Handsome was an understatement for Cisco Mendoza. He was several inches taller than Delaney, with broad shoulders under his dark jacket and crisp white shirt that tapered to a lean waist. His eyes were the richest brown she'd ever seen, and his thick dark hair looked like it had been styled for a photo shoot. She tugged at her bouncy blond curls, which had taken an hour in hot rollers to create but suddenly felt too girlish.

"You two get to know each other." Shannon looked over Delaney's shoulder. "I owe Galen the next dance."

Before Delaney could argue, Shannon had disappeared toward the center of the dance floor.

"It's lovely to meet you," Cisco said, his voice smooth like the finest whiskey. Delaney didn't actually drink whiskey, but that's how she imagined it. Smooth with the subtlest hint of sin.

She realized he was staring at her, waiting for her to answer. One side of his mouth quirked, as if he could see how flustered she felt standing in front of him.

Delaney wasn't thrown off balance very often, and
it made her skin itch. The bodice of her strapless gown
suddenly felt too tight and she struggled to draw in a
normal breath.

"You, too," she said, surprised that her voice was
steady. "It means a lot to Gabi to have her family here. Do
you like Horseback Hollow? How long are you in town?"
She clapped a hand over her mouth to stop the babbling.

Cisco's grin widened, and for a moment Delaney forgot her own name, the fact she was in the barn that felt
like a second home, surrounded by people she'd known
her whole life. All she could see was this man and his
wicked smile.

"It means a great deal to us to be with her on this
day," he said slowly, as if speaking to a child. "I do like
Horseback Hollow, and I'm not sure how long I'll be in
town." He cocked his head as the music started again, a
slow ballad this time.

Delaney tilted her head, mimicking his movement before snapping out of her lust-induced haze. A man like
Cisco was not for her, but something about him...

"Would you care to dance?" he asked softly.

She stared at his outstretched hand, wanting nothing in the world as much as she wanted to step into his
arms. She thought about her hand on that broad shoulder, her nose pressed into his throat. He would smell
wonderful—she had no doubt. She practically burned
with the need to touch him.

"Delaney," he said, a little louder now. "Dance with
me?"

She almost slid her hand into his, allowed him to lead
her onto the dance floor. Her fingers trembled in anticipa-

tion as she lifted them. But at the last minute she pulled her hand tight to her middle.

"Nope, sorry," she said on a ragged breath. "Gotta go." And with that, she turned and ran for the door.

Chapter One

A warm breeze blew across the Texas plains as Cisco Mendoza adjusted his cowboy hat. A thin bead of sweat trailed its way down his back. The temperature remained pleasant so early on this April morning, which meant the sweat was from nerves instead. He rolled his shoulders to force himself to relax.

Cisco didn't do nerves.

Back in Miami, he was known for his ability to manage even the most contentious real estate deals with his signature mix of coolness and charm. But Horseback Hollow, Texas, was a far piece from South Florida. Still, a deal was a deal and if Cisco was good at one thing in his life, it was closing the deal.

"This project takes vision," he said to the man standing next to him. "And we both know Alden Moore has vision. It's one of the ways he's built Moore Entertainment to be the success it is now."

Kent Stephens, the regional VP of Marketing and Development for Moore Entertainment, not to mention Cisco's new boss, nodded. "Mr. Moore has vision, all right, and these condos are a big part of it. He has high expectations for Cowboy Country, but the pushback from the locals in town has become a thorn in all of our sides." He flipped a rock off to the side with the toe of his expensive loafer. "Those Fortunes won't give us a chance and their influence seems to run all the way to Lubbock." He pointed at Cisco. "Which, as we discussed, is where you come in. You've got pull with them and we need you to use it."

"Right." Cisco gave Kent a reassuring smile. "My sister is married to Jude Fortune Jones and you know that branch of the family wields a lot of power around town." Before Kent could respond, Cisco walked back toward his truck, across the open land he planned to help develop into luxury condos. It was true his younger sister, Gabi, had married Jude a couple of months ago right here in town, but as far as the Fortune influence in Horseback Hollow, that was pure guesswork. Jude had a bunch of brothers and sisters plus a horde of Fortune cousins in the area, so Cisco figured he couldn't be too far off the mark.

He'd originally come to Horseback Hollow just for Gabi's wedding, but when he'd heard about Moore's plans to develop the Western-themed amusement park and related real estate, Cisco had decided to stick around. He was busy and successful with his real estate projects in Miami. But recently he'd begun feeling restless and a little bored with the endless stream of business lunches, rounds of golf and nights spent with the who's who of South Beach. He loved his life but attributed his change in attitude to a childhood spent moving from place to place as his family followed his father's career in the air force. Cisco wasn't the type of guy to put down roots, and he always enjoyed the thrill of a new challenge.

Too bad his expertise in Miami didn't mean much to his new bosses in Horseback Hollow. What had been more important to them was his connection to the influential Fortune family—a connection that was tenuous at best. Gabi loved her new in-laws, and his father, Orlando, seemed a bit smitten with Josephine Fortune Chesterfield, the matriarch of the British branch of the clan. Cisco hadn't gotten close to any of the Fortunes personally, something he knew was going to need to change quickly.

"When can we get a meeting on the books with your Fortune friends?" Kent followed him across the empty field. "Cowboy Country is scheduled to open next month, and Mr. Moore wants to break ground on the condos by the end of the summer. The condos are new territory for Moore Entertainment, so we want outside investors to support this project. They need to be lined up in short order and catching a Fortune will go a long way toward attracting other important players around this part of Texas."

Cisco glanced over his shoulder at the other man. Moore Entertainment had bought this huge tract of land near the planned amusement park for the express purpose of developing condos to expand the Cowboy Country brand. From what Cisco could tell, Kent was a decent guy, in his late fifties and totally devoted to his job. He'd relocated to Horseback Hollow from Chicago to dedicate his time exclusively to Cowboy Country. Cisco knew Kent had a lot riding on the success of this venture. Everyone at Moore Entertainment did.

"I'll bring you the investors." Cisco kept his answer purposefully vague. "Closing the deal is my specialty."

"As long as the Fortunes are part of the deal, we're all good." Kent opened the trunk of his expensive BMW and pulled out a roll of paper. He closed the trunk, then spread the sheets across the gleaming black surface. Cisco had to give the guy credit—it was no easy feat to keep a car so clean with all the dust out on the plains of Texas. For the next twenty minutes, they discussed the plans for the Cowboy Condos, including a marketing strategy and target market. Cisco had his first niggling of doubt as he looked at drawings of stucco buildings with windows shaped like boots. He was used to dealing with extremely upscale developments and while Moore was certainly sinking a bunch of money into this project, the designs didn't yet have the spark Cisco knew they would need to appeal to high-end investors. Right now, the Cowboy Condos reminded him of a kitschy motel off the highway. He wanted to turn them into a Western-themed Ritz.

Kent seemed willing to take his advice and input. The Mendozas had roots in Texas, so Cisco capitalized on his family history to encourage some authentic Western additions to the project. By the time the other man rolled up the plans, Cisco felt more confident things would work out in this deal. He would make sure they did, no matter what he had to do to get the end result he needed.

He watched Kent drive away, then turned to climb in the truck he'd leased from a dealership in nearby Vicker's Corners. As he did, he noticed a lone horseback rider in the distance, tearing across the land, horse and rider clearly in sync as the horse's hooves thundered over the ground. He felt his mouth go dry and had to remind himself to take a breath. That was a real cowboy, or maybe a cowboy kid, by the size of the rider. Cisco knew enough about horses and the West to pass himself off as a cowboy to his coworkers at Moore Entertainment, but this rider was the real deal from the tip of his cowboy hat to the glint of the metal on his saddle. Talk about a thrill. He was too far away to be noticed, but he stood and watched until the horse disappeared behind an outcropping of rocks, leaving a trail of dust in its wake.

That was the kind of adrenaline rush Cisco had been missing in his life, and he hoped pushing through this deal on the Cowboy Condos would reignite the fire that he'd been seeking.

Climbing into a booth across from his sister, Gabi, at the Horseback Hollow Grill an hour later, Cisco decided there was no time like the present to start making his future dream a reality.

"How's it going, Mrs. Fortune Jones?" he asked with a wink. "I hope that husband of yours knows how lucky he is to have you and treats you accordingly. He'll have big brother to answer to if not."

Gabi rolled her eyes, but Cisco saw her mouth curve into a reluctant smile. "Jude and I keep each other happy," she said. "I'm really glad you came in for the wedding and that you've stayed, Cisco."

For a moment he forgot his reason for wanting to speak with his sister and took the time to enjoy the pleasure of her company. As the only girl in a family of four boisterous boys, Gabriella was always special, but her big heart and sweet soul made her even more so. It was good to reconnect with her now that he was in Horseback Hollow.

"It's a cool town," he answered. "For now, anyway."

"Speaking of, what are your plans? The Cisco I know

is always moving, working an angle or the next big deal. Do you plan to stay long enough to find a job here?"

He made the conscious effort not to cringe at her question. He hadn't actually told anyone in his family that he was working for Moore Entertainment on the Cowboy Condos. It had quickly become clear his sister and father weren't overly thrilled about the amusement park's presence in town. He didn't want to open himself up to their comments just yet.

"I've got some irons in the fire," he said, avoiding a direct answer. "I also have loose ends to wrap up on a couple of Miami projects." He paused as a waitress stopped by the table, giving him a friendly smile as she took their orders. He wiggled his eyebrows at Gabi as the young woman walked away. "Either way, I bet I can keep myself busy."

Gabi blew out a frustrated breath. "Someday you're going to find the right woman, Cisco."

"I've found a lot of right women, Gabriella. Why limit it to one?"

"Because you have a huge heart under all that macho bravado." She wagged a finger at him. "You're more than a skirt chaser. Mama would have wanted you to find someone special."

A place in his chest ached at the mention of their mother. Luz Mendoza had died three years ago. She'd been the heart and soul of their family and Cisco knew Gabrielle and their brothers still felt the loss of her as much as he did.

"Dad seems happy in Horseback Hollow," he said, trying to subtly change the subject.

He figured Gabi was wise to his tactic, but she played

along. "He fits here. It's given him a way to feel a part of the community and taken away some of his loneliness."

"He seems to be pretty close to some of the Fortunes, as well."

Gabi nodded. "They're a wonderful family. In fact, Jude's parents, Jeanne Marie and Deke, are having a barbecue out at their ranch this weekend. I'm sure they'd love for you to join the fun. It would mean a lot to me for you to get to know Jude and his family."

Cisco did an internal fist pump. He'd meet more of the Fortunes and make his sister happy in the process. Nothing like multitasking. "That sounds great. Text me their address and the details on when to be there."

"I will."

"I've been hearing a lot about the new amusement park in the works. They call it Cowboy Country, right?"

Gabi's smile dimmed. "I wouldn't bring that up at the barbecue. Most of the Fortunes aren't too pleased about it."

Cisco took a casual sip of coffee. "Really? Why?"

"A lot of locals like Horseback Hollow just the way it is," Gabi told him. "Besides, from everything I hear, the company in charge doesn't care about the history of the area. The place is hokey and utterly lacking any authenticity. People around here take the cowboy lifestyle seriously. It's not just a carnival show to be exploited."

"But won't it mean more jobs?"

His sister shrugged. "True, but the cost of that sort of progress may be more than Horseback Hollow wants to pay."

"So are all the Fortunes against it?" Cisco's gut felt as if it had taken a direct hit with a sledgehammer.

"Jude thinks it's an awful idea and so do his parents.

In fact, I'd say the only member of the family who's the least bit excited about it is Delaney, Jude's baby sister."

"Delaney," Cisco repeated quietly, trying to picture her from the wedding. "Tiny thing, lots of blond hair?"

"That's her, but add in a thousand-watt smile and the energy to match. The topic of Cowboy Country came up at dinner a couple of weeks ago, and Delaney mentioned she thinks the park might be fun. She's a total sweetheart, but Horseback Hollow is all she knows. I think she wants a little adventure in her life." Gabi cocked her head, looking at her brother. "And why are you interested in Cowboy Country, anyway?"

He busied himself with adding cream to his coffee, avoiding his sister's shrewd gaze. "Just want to keep up on the local business news. And if Delaney Fortune is looking for adventure…"

"No way, Cisco. She's not your type of girl."

"What's my type?"

"Brainless and shallow," Gabi snapped.

He'd made the comment to sidetrack her but had to admit his sister's assessment of his taste in women stung.

Gabriella's smile turned sympathetic. "Speaking of women, Matteo and Rachel will probably stop by the barbecue for a bit. Are you okay with that?"

Before Cisco could answer, the waitress brought their food. As she put the plate down in front of him, she also slipped a piece of paper under the edge. "You're new to town, right?"

"All the way from Miami," he said with a practiced smile.

"Give me a call sometime," she answered. "I can show you the sights."

Gabi let out a delicate snort. "Horseback Hollow doesn't have 'sights.'"

The waitress ignored her. "Call me," she whispered to Cisco, then turned on her heel, her hips swaying gently as she headed back toward the restaurant's kitchen.

Cisco's smile widened as he gave his sister a quick wink. "I'm happy for Matteo. He and Rachel are great together." Before his younger brother had claimed Rachel Robinson, Cisco had gone on a date with her, more to spark Matteo into action than because of any deep feelings between Cisco and Rachel. "You know I'm not going to settle down anytime soon, Gabi. It's not who I am."

His sister only studied him, a knowing smile playing at the corner of her mouth. "Famous last words, Cisco. Famous last words."

"I'm here, Mom." Delaney Fortune Jones rushed into the kitchen of the house she'd been born and raised in, snagging a chocolate-chip cookie from the counter as she did. Her parents were hosting one of their big family barbecues tonight, so there would be plenty to be done to get ready.

"Put the cookie down and wash your hands, young lady." Her mother, Jeanne Marie Fortune Jones, had her back turned toward Delaney as she reached in the pantry. Delaney was pretty sure her mother had eyes in the back of her head, not to mention some psychic ability. She seemed to always know exactly what was going on with each of her children no matter where they were.

At twenty-four, Delaney was the youngest and the only one still living with her parents, but she was in no hurry to move into a place of her own. She loved her childhood home and the hustle and bustle that went with living on a working ranch.

"Sorry I'm late." She set the cookie on a paper towel and turned to the sink. "I went for a ride after I helped the guys secure the fencing near the west border and lost track of time. But I'm here to help with whatever you need."

Jeanne Marie turned, holding a large ceramic bowl in her arms. "It's under control, sweetie. No worries. There's still plenty left to get ready. You can help dish out the potato salad after you shower. We'll need plates and napkins ready to go. And there's a big pitcher of sun tea brewing on the back porch."

"Potato salad, plates and tea." Delaney flipped off the water, dried her hands on the paper towel, then took a bite of cookie. "These are so good, Mom. As always."

"It doesn't take much to please your sweet tooth," her mother answered with a smile. "I'm sure Angie will bring her brownies, so save some room."

Delaney patted her stomach. "I always have room for dessert. Besides, riding makes me extra hungry."

"You've been out on longer rides than usual this week. What's going on?"

"Flapjack has been restless," Delaney answered before popping the rest of the cookie into her mouth. She went to the cabinet where her mother kept the paper plates and wicker holders for them and began stacking things on the counter. "I wanted to give him some extra exercise."

"He's not the only one who's been restless." Jeanne Marie's soft arms came around Delaney's waist as her mother rested her chin on Delaney's shoulder. "I know it's been difficult for you now that most of your siblings are partnered off."

Delaney leaned back against her mother, breathing in Jeanne Marie's familiar sweet smell. "It's just Galen and me left now. I'm happy for the rest of them, but it makes things…different. Good, but different."

"You'll find the right man, Delaney. You're an amazing woman with so much to give."

"Spoken like a true doting mother." Jeanne Marie stepped back and Delaney turned with a smile. "I know the perfect guy is out there for me, and I'm not in a hurry. I want what you and Daddy have. I love Horseback Hollow, and I'm going to find someone who values this town and the lifestyle that comes with it as much as I do."

"Well, your brothers all have friends."

"Who see me as their baby sister." Delaney wrinkled her nose. "That's just weird." She reached behind her and unfastened the clip holding up her two braids. She'd taken to pinning up her long hair under her hat as she rode to keep it out of the sun and wind. "You never know— maybe the amusement park will attract some new cowboys to Horseback Hollow."

"None of any substance," Jeanne Marie said through her teeth. "I don't understand your fascination with that development, Delaney. It's a thorn in the side to most of the town."

"Not to everyone," she countered. "Amber Rogers is working with them, and Wendy and Marcus Mendoza can't be too unhappy with the additional business for the Cantina. Maybe everyone has been too quick to judge Cowboy Country. Did you ever think of that?"

"I haven't," her mother admitted with a rueful smile. She gave Delaney another quick hug. "You have such a beautiful heart, my girl. I look forward to the day you find a man who will value it as much as I do."

Chapter Two

Delaney came down the steps from her bedroom two hours later, putting her still-wet hair into a braid that trailed past her shoulders. The barbecue was already in full swing. As usual, there had been plenty of ranch chores to sidetrack her. After helping her mom she'd found her father in the barn feeding afternoon hay to the horses. Delaney loved nothing more than spending time with her dad, especially with the sweet, musty scent of the barn surrounding them.

Deke Jones was a quiet, sometimes crusty rancher and his relationships with his children, especially Delaney's brother Christopher, hadn't always been easy. But Delaney felt like she understood her dad and his stoic devotion to the land and his work, so his long silences and gruff tone had never bothered her much. So many of her good memories from childhood centered around life on the ranch. She knew that was part of the reason she felt so strongly about creating her own life in and around Horseback Hollow.

But as her gaze trailed across the crowd of family and friends gathered in the house and spilling out to the back porch and yard, her breath caught in her throat. There was no doubt she loved her large, boisterous family, and her brothers and sister had all made excellent matches in love. But the overabundance of couples and kids made her feel the tiniest bit wistful for a love of her own. It was silly, she knew. Delaney had always been the bubbly, happy-go-lucky kid in her family. She was in no hurry to settle down, but she'd always been a part of a group. As the youngest of seven, she'd never truly been alone. While her brothers and sister focused on their new families, she was suddenly left on her own and it didn't sit well.

"Would you take this plate of fruit out to the tables?" her mother's voice called from the kitchen.

Delaney made her smile especially bright, although she didn't think for a moment that fooled Jeanne Marie and her laser-sharp instinct for her children's moods.

"I remember the year Stacey finally went off to kindergarten and you were left alone here," Jeanne Marie said as she handed Delaney the ceramic platter. "You got into more trouble that school year than all the other kids combined when they were little."

"I'm not a little girl anymore," Delaney offered. "I can handle this."

"I know you can, sweetheart." Her mother absently touched the turquoise pendant around her throat. "But you have a tendency to get reckless when you're bored. I wouldn't be doing my job as a mother if I didn't worry over you."

"I love you, Mom." Delaney placed a light kiss on her mother's cheek. "You go enjoy the party. I'll take this plate out and make sure everything else is running smoothly."

Jeanne Marie nodded and Delaney followed her into the backyard. She greeted her brothers and their wives and girlfriends, plus Stacey and her new husband, Colton, on the way. After she set down the fruit, several of her nieces and nephews came running up and she was once again lost in the happiness of her large family. She forgot about her restlessness and feeling alone in the midst of so much love and affection.

"These gatherings just keep getting bigger."

She turned as her brother Liam walked up. He was followed by another brother, Toby, who handed her a glass of lemonade.

"It makes Mom and Dad happy to have all the kids running around again."

"It makes me happy to have mine occupied by something other than making a mess for Angie and me to clean up."

Delaney punched him lightly on the shoulder. "You're not fooling me," she said. "You're the biggest softy in the world and those three kids are amazing." Toby had taken in three foster children last year and then adopted Brian, Justin and Kylie, making a home for them along with his new bride, Angie. They were a wonderful family. Delaney loved seeing her brother so content.

"It's a good life," he agreed, grinning. "And between us, Angie left a special plate of brownies on the kitchen counter for you."

"She's the best sister-in-law ever."

"Don't let the others hear you say that," Liam warned in a teasing tone.

Delaney laughed. "They're all the best," she amended quickly. "I'll deny to my grave that I ever said anything else."

It was a beautiful evening, the warmth of the day cooling to the perfect temperature as the sun began to set. The expansive Texas sky turned brilliant shades of orange and pink across the pasture behind her parents' house. Once everyone ate and the food was cleared, her father turned on a movie for the kids and they snuggled up together on the comfy couches and chairs in the large family room. The adults drifted between the kitchen and the back patio, where the talk centered around calving season and the Texans' chances in the upcoming baseball season.

Delaney grabbed a denim jacket off the hook near the kitchen door but found herself lingering at the edge of the gathering as she came back outside. For once, she was almost happy being alone, until a deep voice spoke at her shoulder.

"What's a pretty lady like you doing out here by herself?"

She whirled around to find Cisco Mendoza staring down at her and fought the urge to fidget. Of course she recognized Cisco, since his sister, Gabriella, had married her brother Jude only a couple of months ago. Cisco had come to Horseback Hollow for the wedding and decided to stay in town. She'd met him briefly at the reception, making a complete fool of herself thanks to her body's reaction to all that male perfection. But she couldn't quite figure out why he was still here, since he clearly belonged in trendy South Beach more than her hometown. Even tonight he projected an air of cool sophistication at odds with his relaxed button-down shirt and dark designer jeans. No Wrangler jeans for this guy. It annoyed Delaney that her stomach did a tiny two-step at the way his lean shoulders filled out the expensive silk of his shirt. No one could deny Cisco was gorgeous, but Delaney wasn't interested in a too-hot-for-words guy. She wanted someone strong and steady and doubted Cisco fit the bill.

"I'm not by myself," she countered, trying not to sound breathless. "I'm surrounded by my entire family."

His dark eyes flicked to the people gathered on the farside of the patio. "It was generous of your parents to include me in the party. My sister is lucky to have married into the Fortune family."

"I'd think someone like you would find us a little country bumpkin."

"Like me?"

She waved her hand in front of him. "You're a sophisticated city slicker. All smooth angles and—" she leaned in to sniff him "—expensive cologne."

"You think I smell good?" He gave her a cocky grin.

Delaney huffed out a breath. "Not. The. Point."

"What makes you think I'm such a city slicker? My sister fits in here in Horseback Hollow just fine. My father loves it here."

"You're nothing like Orlando." She touched the tip of one of her red cowboy boots to his. "Your boots aren't even scuffed."

"They're new," he argued.

"*That's* the point," she agreed.

Cisco rocked back on his heels. To Delaney's surprise, instead of looking offended at her comments, he seemed to enjoy her remarks. "Are all the Fortunes as opinionated as you?" he asked, his smile now genuine.

"I'm sorry," she said, surprised to realize she was. Delaney was a positive person, always wanting to see the best in people. She didn't normally give grief to someone she'd just met. "I don't mean to get all up in your face. My mom tells me I seem restless. Maybe that's making me a little prickly."

Cisco stifled a groan as he watched her take a sip of lemonade, her soft pink mouth pressing against the straw. Delaney Fortune Jones could get all up in his face anytime she wanted, he realized with a start. It was strange. Gabriella had been right—the petite blonde in front of him wasn't his usual type. He couldn't deny she was attractive, but it was definitely in a more wholesome way than he was used to. She wore a floral-patterned dress with a wide leather belt cinched around her tiny waist. The collar of the colorful fabric was ruffled and soft, giving him tiny glimpses of the pale skin at the base of her throat. She wore red cowboy boots but even with the heel on them, she was almost six inches shorter than him. A tiny, adorable package of a woman with her long blond braid draped over her shoulder and clear blue eyes. She looked like the kind of woman you took home for Sunday dinner, not wined and dined the way he was used to.

He knew his sister would have his head if he made any wrong moves with Delaney but he couldn't seem to walk away. He told himself it was because he needed to reel in a Fortune for his job with Moore Entertainment. That was simpler than examining any other possibility.

"I don't mind prickly." He took a slow pull on his beer and let his eyes wander up and down her petite figure. "Especially not when the lady in question is as pretty as you."

To his surprise, she poked him in the chest with one

slender finger. "Don't do that. Don't try to smooth-talk me, Cisco Mendoza. You might be God's gift to women but that doesn't mean I'm practicing your particular brand of religion."

His mouth dropped open in shock for a moment before he managed to snap it shut again. He rubbed the center of his chest and placed his beer bottle on a nearby table. It was only his second drink, but maybe the alcohol was hitting him harder than he thought. Never in his life had Cisco had a problem charming a woman. Even when he was a boy, his brothers would be angry with him for sweet-talking himself out of class assignments. The fact was Cisco had a way with the ladies, and he didn't mind exploiting that gift when it suited him. But now he needed to get in Delaney Fortune Jones's good graces and was making a total mess of the conversation.

He decided his only choice was to lay the truth on the line and go from there. "You are pretty," he began, holding his hands up, palms forward, when she narrowed her eyes. Even if Delaney was immune to his charm, her natural beauty couldn't be ignored. "But the fact is I need a Fortune. The kind with a capital *F*. And I need one yesterday."

She waved toward her parents' back patio. "There are plenty to choose from. Why is a Fortune so important to you?"

"I'm working on a business deal," he said, giving her the truth even if it wasn't the whole story. "I can't share details yet, but we need investors. My bosses know I have a connection to the Fortune family through Gabriella."

"The Fortune Jones family," Delaney clarified. "There's a big difference."

"How big?"

"A-lot-of-zeros big."

He tried not to look shocked but must have failed, because she chuckled. "James Marshall Fortune, my mother's long-lost brother, tried to give her money, but she returned it. We Jones kids had a totally normal life here in Horseback Hollow. My dad is the best. He works hard and made sacrifices for his family, but no one in my branch of the family has the money of the Red Rock or Atlanta Fortunes. We took the Fortune name to honor my mom and her connection to her relatives, not to cash in on their wealth."

"That's...honorable," Cisco told her, suddenly wishing he had done a bit more research into the Fortunes of Horseback Hollow before making promises to Cowboy Country.

"But if you need a Fortune for a meeting, I might be able to make some time in my schedule. Jude is definitely out because of calving season, even if Gabi asked him for the favor. I'm not sure any of my other siblings would be up for it. You'd be stuck with me."

He studied her but she seemed to be sincere. "I'd be grateful."

"I have conditions." Delaney gave him a wide grin.

He couldn't help but return her smile. It was infectious. "Lay them on me, *cielo*."

"I want you to get your boots dirty."

It was his turn to narrow his eyes. "What does that mean exactly?"

"Spend time with me out here. Our home is a working ranch." She did a small twirl as her hands waved toward the expanse of fields behind the house and the large barn to one side. "I want to put you through the paces to see if you can handle what it means to be a Fortune Jones."

The crisp, summery scent of her wafted over him as she moved. He wasn't sure if it was her perfume or shampoo, but it made his senses reel. Cisco felt himself drifting closer to Delaney, as if pulled by an invisible thread of curiosity. She was so different from any woman he'd met before, completely authentic and pure, as if she was untainted by life. It was also obvious she loved life on the ranch. While he tried to live by his own code of right and wrong, the deals he brokered often left him walking a moral tightrope. It had been years since Cisco had felt anything close to innocent. He found that quality in Delaney intensely attractive.

But this was business, he reminded himself.

As if to drive home the point, his sister suddenly appeared at Delaney's side.

"What are you two talking about so intently?" she asked with a bright smile for Delaney and a warning glance at Cisco.

"Delaney is going to teach me how to be a real cowboy," Cisco told his sister.

He expected her to laugh or make a joke about how he wouldn't be able to handle it, but she stepped forward and gave him a hug. "I think it's a great idea." She turned to Delaney. "It's about time he broke a sweat in someplace other than a fancy gym."

"You wound me," Cisco said with a laugh. "For your information, there are plenty of times I've broken a sweat outside of a gym."

Gabriella rolled her eyes when he winked. "Don't go there, big brother." She linked her arm in Delaney's. "Let's join the others. The desserts are going fast, Delaney. There's a brownie with your name on it."

Cisco followed the two women back toward the rest of the guests, although he realized he would have been happy to keep Delaney all to himself for a while longer.

Apparently he'd have more time to spend with her as he met her criteria for taking the meeting with the executives from Cowboy Country. He just had to come up with a plan to hold them off in the meantime.

"How about this one?"

Cisco grimaced as his father held up a garish Western shirt decorated with rhinestones and leather tassels. "Now you're just being cruel, Dad. I may not be an expert on cowboys, but I can tell you no self-respecting man would wear that in public."

"You'd be surprised," Orlando answered with a chuckle. "But we'll start you out subtle. After all, Deke Jones is going to expect you to look like you can handle yourself before he lets you do anything on his ranch."

Like Gabi, Orlando had been all for Cisco spending time with Delaney at her family's ranch. His brother Matteo had found it hilarious to imagine Cisco doing any sort of hard physical labor. That irritated him. Sure, his experience was brokering big-time deals, but it didn't mean he couldn't get his hands dirty. There might not be a lot of opportunity for that in Miami, but Cisco was confident he could hold his own.

Unfortunately, his wardrobe didn't lend itself to ranching. In Miami the style was South Beach cool, silk shirts and trousers or polo shirts for the golf course. He didn't want to look as green as he really was in front of Delaney's father, so he'd asked his dad where to shop for Western clothes. Orlando had insisted on accompanying him to nearby Vicker's Corners to pick up some new, more Horseback Hollow–appropriate clothes.

In the end they kept it simple—a few button-downs, one plaid with pearl buttons and two of solid colors, a few pairs of Wrangler and Cinch jeans, and a belt with a three-piece buckle.

They walked out of the store and threw the purchases in the backseat of Cisco's truck before grabbing sandwiches from a local street vendor. Orlando led Cisco to a bench in a nearby park. It was good to spend time with his father and great to see how healthy and happy Orlando looked. He'd been nearly killed last year when the plane he was piloting crashed but now seemed to be back to his old hale and hearty self.

"Your mother would get a kick out of us shopping together," Orlando said as he unwrapped his sandwich.

"I'm not sure she'd believe it." Cisco took a drink of iced tea. "I'm not sure *I* believe it." He reached over and patted his father's shoulder. "But it's good to see you so happy, Dad. Mom would have wanted that."

The breeze blew through his father's thick silver hair. "I miss her every day, son, but you're right. She wouldn't have wanted any of us to put our lives on hold and wallow in grief. Gabriella found her happiness, and it appears Matteo has, too. Now it's your turn. Horseback Hollow is a good place for the Mendozas."

"Whoa," Cisco said quickly, his head shaking. "I don't disagree the town is great, but I'm not looking to settle down like Gabi and Matteo. My life is in Miami. There are some business opportunities in Texas, and I'm going to take advantage of them. That's all it is."

Orlando opened his mouth to answer just as his cell phone beeped. He checked the screen, then punched at the keys with his thumbs, a small smile playing across his lips.

"Are you texting?" Cisco smiled around a bite of sandwich. It was grilled chicken with avocado on thick buttered toast and one of the best things Cisco had tasted in months. He ate out almost every night in Miami, often at trendy restaurants with clients, but somehow the down-home food in this area was infinitely more satisfying.

"I may be old, but I'm not dead."

Something about the look on his father's face gave Cisco pause. "Are you texting a *woman*?"

Orlando kept hitting keys on his phone, but as he pressed Send and looked up, Cisco noticed color rising up his neck. "That's none of your concern."

"Do you have a girlfriend, Dad?"

"I loved your mother very much, Cisco. I was devoted to her for all our years together. You know that." Orlando pocketed his phone and concentrated on his sandwich.

"I know how much you loved Mom," Cisco agreed, choosing his words carefully. "And how difficult it was when she died. But she'd want you to keep living. If you've met someone who makes you happy, I support you, Dad. We all will."

Orlando looked at him a long moment, then nodded. "You're a good boy, son."

"So who is she?" Cisco nudged his father's arm. "Are you officially dating? When do I get to meet her? Do we need to have the 'be safe and responsible' talk?"

"You're a good boy who needs to mind his own business." Orlando wadded up the paper from his sandwich. "Don't worry about me. You just straighten out your own life."

"My life is fantastic." Cisco realized the words sounded more defensive than he'd meant.

"There's more to life than work."

"I understand, but I'm also building a career," Cisco answered, irritation flaring through him. "You took your career in the air force very seriously."

"Of course I did," his father agreed. "But I had your mother and you kids, as well. It was a lot to juggle, and I know it wasn't always easy on our family."

"I didn't mind it."

His father chuckled. "You had a gift, Cisco. You could go into any school, any group of kids and make your mark within minutes. You were the leader of every situation. I've never met a kid with so much confidence."

Cisco hadn't thought of it that way as a kid. He'd been intent on survival. As "military brats" of Latino heritage, the Mendoza kids had definitely made an impression wherever they went. He'd felt as if it were his job to make sure the impression was a good one. He'd had a natural gift for influencing people that had served him well both as a boy and later as he started his career. Plus, he always liked a challenge, which was part of the reason he'd taken the job at Cowboy Country. His reputation in Miami was solid. It was time he made a name for himself in other areas.

"You and Mom set the bar high," he told his father, standing and taking their trash to a nearby garbage can. "I'll get there, Papi, don't worry. But right now I'm focused on business." Still, an image of Delaney and her cornflower-blue eyes popped into his mind. He shook off the mental picture.

"I know you will, son." Orlando gave him a knowing smile. "You're a Mendoza. We're built for true love."

Cisco wasn't sure he agreed, but he didn't argue. Right now all he wanted was to make this deal with the Cowboy Condos a success and move on to even larger projects. Texas was a big state, and he intended to conquer every inch of it.

Chapter Three

"Stop fidgeting." Jeanne Marie took a pan of freshly baked blueberry muffins out of the oven. She turned to Delaney as she took the pot holders off her hands. "You look beautiful."

Delaney huffed out a breath, annoyed as her stomach took another tumble. "I'm not trying to look beautiful." She smoothed her palms down the faded denim of her shirt. "I'll be working today and Cisco Mendoza is going to help."

"He's quite handsome."

"Right," Delaney said with a laugh. "Mom, saying Cisco is handsome is like saying Texas is hot in the summer."

"Kind of an understatement?"

"Exactly." She snagged a muffin from the cooling rack and bounced it in her hand until it cooled enough to take a bite. "I can't image a woman not being attracted to Cisco. It doesn't matter. I want a man with substance over style."

"Who says you can't have both? Your father was—and still is—the most handsome man I've ever seen."

Delaney shook her head. "I'm not looking for anything from Cisco but some good old-fashioned hard labor. Like you said, I get into trouble when I'm bored. He's a diversion. Nothing more."

"You can at least enjoy getting to know him. He comes from a wonderful family. You know how much we all love Gabriella, and Orlando is a good man. In fact, your aunt Josephine seems quite taken with him."

"Aunt Josephine and Orlando Mendoza?" Delaney didn't know her British aunt well but already felt a connection to her. "That's kind of sweet."

Jeanne Marie smiled. "Keep this between us. If there is something happening between the two of them, they should have the time to figure it out for themselves."

"Of course." It was strange for Delaney to imagine her sophisticated aunt being with a salt-of-the-earth man like Orlando. She had a picture in her mind of who people should fit with and for her it was always someone from a similar background. A man who'd been raised for the cowboy lifestyle—working hard and loving the land—just as she had. She wondered now if that was narrow-minded, something Delaney had never thought about herself.

It wasn't a help for her already jumbled nerves, but she didn't have much time to examine those feelings as she heard a truck rumble down the driveway.

"Have fun," Jeanne Marie told her, wrapping up two more muffins in a napkin. "And take these to your new man. He's going to need the energy for what I imagine you have planned."

Delaney grabbed the napkin and gave her mother a quick kiss. She did, indeed, have plans for Cisco. The thought of the fun she was going to have with him turned her nerves into excitement.

The roller coaster in her tummy went dipping and twisting again as Cisco climbed out of his truck. She was pleasantly surprised to see he'd shed his sophisticated Miami clothes and this morning looked like a true Texas cowboy in his plaid shirt, crisp jeans and sturdy leather cowboy boots. Even his hat looked custom-fit, the sort of hat any of her brothers would be proud to wear.

"You cowboy up pretty nicely, Mr. Mendoza."

"Thank you, Ms. Fortune Jones. I'm honored to be here." He reached into his truck and pulled out a pair of leather work gloves and a small gift bag. "These are for me," he said, slapping the gloves against his thigh. "This is for you." He held out the gift bag.

Delaney looked over her shoulder toward the house. For a moment she wondered if her mother or one of her siblings had told Cisco about her weakness for presents. As the youngest of seven, Delaney had been the recipient of countless hand-me-downs. Clothes from her sister, Stacey, and saddles from her brothers. Her parents had always made her birthday special, but that came around only once a year and it wasn't nearly enough to satisfy her.

"You didn't have to—" she began, then stopped when she noticed Cisco grinning at her. "But I'm glad you did."

She pulled a piece of folded tissue paper out of the bag and unwrapped it. Inside was a delicate gold chain with a small charm in the shape of the state of Texas hanging from the end.

"I hope you don't have one like it," Cisco said. "I saw it in a store in Vicker's Corners and it reminded me of you."

"It's adorable." Delaney cleared her throat when the words came out in a whisper. "I love it." She did, too. The necklace was perfect for her. She wasn't sure whether that meant she should trust Cisco's taste or be wary of how smooth of a charmer he could be.

"May I put it on you?" The deep rumble of his voice brought her out of her musings.

She nodded but didn't release the necklace. "Why did you get this for me?"

A look of surprise flashed across his face. "You're doing me a big favor, Delaney. I wanted to thank you."

"I haven't done anything yet," she countered.

"A thank-you in advance?" His smile was genuine.

She uncurled her fingers from the chain and dropped it into his palm. "Are you sure you're not trying to get me to go easy on you?" She turned and lifted her braid out of the way as he reached his hands in front of her.

"Would it work?" His breath was warm on her neck.

As he spoke, he used one finger to push a stray strand of hair out of the way. A ripple of awareness shot down her spine in response. She shook her head a tiny bit, not trusting her voice.

"Then put me through the paces, Delaney." He clasped the necklace together and turned her to face him. "I'm all yours."

Delaney tried to ignore the satisfying warmth that traveled through her at his words. A man like Cisco wasn't for her, she reminded herself. This wasn't his real life. He didn't belong in Horseback Hollow even if he'd shown up this morning looking the part. His boots might be sturdy, but they were brand-new.

By midday his boots were already broken in, along with the rest of him. When Cisco had told Delaney to put him through the paces, he hadn't realized what he was asking. As he loaded a final bale of hay onto a truck in one of the far pastures at the ranch, every part of his body ached. This was definitely different from a five-mile run around South Beach and an hour at the gym. The sun shone high in the western sky, spreading patterns of golden light through the clouds.

They'd been working steadily since the morning. Delaney had saddled up a couple of horses first thing, and they'd started their day checking the fencing on the north end of the ranch. Cisco could hold his own on a horse, but Delaney rode as though she'd been born in a saddle. As he closed up the truck's gate, the ranch hand behind the wheel gave a short wave and the truck slowly made its way back toward the barn.

He lifted his hat off his head and wiped one sleeve across his brow. It felt as if the temperature had risen several degrees just in the past hour.

"How are you holding up?" Delaney asked as she hoisted herself on the large horse she road. She looked more amused than concerned.

Cisco swung his leg into the saddle. "I'll survive," he said with a smile. "I knew running a ranching operation was a lot of work, but I didn't appreciate how much until today." He brought his horse to the side of hers. "The men have a lot of respect for you, Delaney."

It was true. Deke Jones had greeted them on their way to the barn earlier this morning, but Delaney's father had been heading to Lubbock to check out some new equipment. He hadn't officially put Delaney in charge in his absence, but it had been clear the ranch workers looked to her for guidance.

She was a mighty force wrapped up in an adorably tiny package.

"My dad keeps this place running like clockwork. The men know what they're supposed to do without much input from me. My brothers used to help out quite a bit but they've all got their own lives and families now. Well, Galen doesn't have a family, but he's busy."

"Don't downplay your role on the ranch."

For the first time, she looked really flustered. "I'm not, but I think you're giving me more credit than I deserve."

"Or maybe, *cielo*, you give yourself less."

Her eyes tracked to his for a moment and he saw a rare flash of uncertainty there. He realized Delaney Fortune Jones might not be as sure of herself as she led people to believe.

She looked up to the blue sky then, holding her straw cowboy hat to her head. "Let's race back. Mom wants us to eat lunch with her and she'll have it ready by now."

"Did you just tell the time by looking at the sun?"

A hint of color crept up her cheeks. "It's a habit. I don't wear a watch when I'm out on the property." She adjusted the horse's reins in her hands. "Ready?"

He nodded and gave his horse a short kick with his boot heels, but Delaney was already off and running. Cisco didn't bother to try to catch her. Instead he enjoyed the view of her moving across the pasture, the rhythm of her body perfectly matched to the animal beneath her.

When he'd first arrived in Horseback Hollow, he'd missed the BMW coupe he drove in Miami and the sports car's power at his fingertips. Now he realized he'd under-estimated the adrenaline rush of horseback riding. There was something about moving in sync with another living being that beat the excitement of even the fastest engine.

He'd totally forgotten about bringing up the idea of the Cowboy Country condos in casual conversation with Delaney. His plan going into this deal was to drop enough hints about the planned luxury community so she'd be amenable to supporting them when the time came. Instead he'd been so busy keeping up with her he hadn't been able to think of anything else.

That was a mistake he couldn't afford to continue. Cisco had a lot riding on this deal with Moore Entertainment. As delightful as he found Delaney, she wasn't his reason for staying in Horseback Hollow. He had to stick to the plan, make this deal happen and move on to bigger things. He might enjoy women, but Cisco had never let himself get sidetracked by one before. He wasn't going to start now.

Delaney couldn't imagine why she'd ever thought to insist Cisco spend time on the ranch with her. She could barely keep straight in her mind her jobs for the day when he was at her side. That was part of the reason she'd pushed him so hard most of the morning. It helped distract her from her constant reaction to him.

But not enough. Every time he looked at her or gave her that half smile, Delaney got a little weak in the knees. When he was so close she could smell the mix of spice and soap she'd now always associate with Cisco, she couldn't remember her own name, let alone what she was supposed to be doing.

She finished brushing down Flapjack and looked over

to the next stall, where Cisco had groomed the bay she'd given him. Big mistake. His long fingers scratched behind the horse's ears as he bent close to her head, whispering words Delaney couldn't hear. She got an immediate mental image of what it would be like for him to touch her so gently and her body thrummed to life in a way she'd never experienced.

Delaney hadn't exactly set out to "save herself" for the right man, but it seemed to be working out that way. She'd never had a truly serious boyfriend and all of the guys in town were too afraid of her overprotective brothers to look at her as casual fun. Eventually, she'd come to realize she didn't want to be with a man until it felt truly right. She'd always thought her heart would guide her, but watching Cisco made her body want to take the lead.

He looked up at her then and color rushed to her face, although he couldn't possibly read her thoughts. Still, it felt as though his dark eyes saw her in a way no one else had before. Delaney loved how he focused on her even as she reminded herself that this was how Cisco Mendoza operated. He was a lady-killer, and Delaney was sure he could charm any woman with his sexy grin and smoldering eyes. Delaney wasn't special to him, no matter how he made her feel.

"Are you okay?" he asked, as if he could sense her jumbled emotions.

"Fine," she answered quickly, striding out of the stall. "Just hungry. We can wash up at the house and see if Mom needs any help."

He looked as if he wanted to question her further but simply followed her across the driveway and up the steps to the kitchen.

"You two were busy this morning," Jeanne Marie commented as she came into the kitchen.

"Just a normal day," Delaney said, throwing her mother a pointed look as Cisco turned on the water at the kitchen sink to wash his hands.

"If you say so, sweetie." Her mother must have realized how hard Delaney had been pushing Cisco this morning, but she didn't mention it outright. "I'm sure you've both worked up an appetite."

"Thank you for having me to lunch, Mrs. Fortune Jones." Cisco dried his hands on a towel and gave her mother that killer smile.

Delaney watched as her mother fluttered her fingers near her throat. Clearly no woman was immune to that smile. "Call me Jeanne Marie. I'm happy to have you here. The house is quiet now that Delaney's the only one left at the ranch. I miss having a big crowd around all the time."

Delaney finished washing her hands and walked over to give her mom a hug. Today Jeanne Marie wore a pale yellow shirt, long faded denim skirt and her favorite turquoise necklace around her throat. "Be careful what you wish for, Mama. You'll have them dropping off the grandkids all the time."

"You love a busy house as much as I do." Her mother gave her a gentle squeeze, then picked up a plate of sandwiches. "When Delaney was a little girl, she told us she planned to have a dozen children. She wanted her own football team."

"Mom," Delaney said, shaking her head. "That was a long time ago."

"I come from a big family, too," Cisco said as he took the pitcher of lemonade and followed them into the dining room. "Having three brothers and Gabi was a help with the way we moved around for my father's career in the air force. We were a pack and could watch out for each other."

"Does that mean you want lots of kids, too?" Jeanne Marie posed the question casually, then laughed as Cisco's eyes went wide. "I'm only teasing. Come and sit down, Cisco. Tell me about what you think of Horseback Hollow so far."

"It's quiet compared to what I'm used to in Miami," he said as he took the seat Jeanne Marie indicated across from her.

As Delaney slid into the chair next to him, she couldn't help but wonder if *quiet* was another word for boring.

"But there's a definite charm to it," he continued. "You don't easily find places anymore where most everyone knows each other. I understand why my dad and sister feel so at home here."

"Horseback Hollow is a special place," Delaney's mother agreed. "There's a lot of history and tradition in this town. Which is why it's so upsetting to have those Cowboy Country outsiders coming in with their gaudy theme park."

Out of the corner of her eye Delaney noticed Cisco's fingers tighten around his glass.

"It might not be so bad," Delaney said quickly. "The rides look fun and it will give people around here something new to do as entertainment."

"That's one of the problems." Jeanne Marie took a sip of lemonade. "Local folks aren't the ones Cowboy Country is trying to attract. Those people haven't given one thought to how this is going to affect life here or what it even means to be a real cowboy. The whole theme is the

Wild West but all they're planning is some commercialized, demeaning version of it."

"Won't the influx of money be good for the town?" Cisco asked as he picked up his sandwich. "I'd think Horseback Hollow could benefit from additional resources."

"Not if it means giving up our simple way of life," Jeanne Marie told him.

"Just because change comes to Horseback Hollow doesn't mean it has to change the people who live here." His dark gaze went from Delaney to her mother. "When you found out you were related to the Fortunes, that was a big change. Did it change who you are on the inside?"

"Not at all," Delaney answered quickly. "He has a point, Mom."

"We were a solid family before I knew I was a Fortune," Jeanne Marie said with a nod of her head. "But I'm not sure the entire town can withstand the influence of Cowboy Country and the people who might come with it." She turned to Delaney. "As a matter of fact, your father and I were talking about your rides to where they're building. We think you should stop that, Delaney. The opening is just around the corner, so there's too much activity out that way."

There were moments when Delaney loved the feeling of safety that came from being part of a large family and moments when she was stifled by her parents' overprotectiveness.

"You've been visiting Cowboy Country?" Cisco asked.

"A few times a week I take my horse out toward the land around the amusement park to see the progress. It's a good stretch of land for riding."

She saw his mouth drop open. "That was—" He

stopped himself and shook his head. "I agree with your mother. It doesn't seem like a good idea."

"I'm not a kid," Delaney said, aware she sounded petulant.

"We only want what's best for you," Jeanne Marie said quietly.

"I know, Mama." Delaney stabbed a grape with her fork. "I'll be careful." She glanced down at her watch. "We need to get back to work. We're supposed to meet the guys at the lower pasture in a few minutes to finish some repairs on the fence."

"Thank you for another wonderful meal," Cisco said as he stood.

"I hope you can join us again." Jeanne Marie led them back to the kitchen. "We spent the whole time talking about Cowboy Country." She set her plate on the counter and turned to Cisco. "I still want to hear more about your plans in Horseback Hollow. I wouldn't want you to think we're against new people coming to town. We just want to make sure they're here for the right reasons. Like you and your family, Cisco."

Cisco's shoulders stiffened but he gave her mother a warm smile. "Thank you, Jeanne Marie." He took her mother's hand and brushed a soft kiss on her knuckles as he gave her an almost courtly bow. "Your hospitality is matched only by your beauty."

Delaney watched as her practical, old-fashioned mother blushed like a schoolgirl. "It was my pleasure. You're welcome to join us anytime. In fact, Deke and I would love to have you over for dinner one of these nights. We don't get a lot of time for individual visiting during our family barbecues. It isn't often Delaney brings a boy home."

"Oh, my gosh," Delaney said with a gasp. "We're getting back to work now." She grabbed on to Cisco's arm and tugged him toward the door. "Let's go, Cisco."

She dragged him, laughing, into the midday sun.

"It's okay, Delaney," he said when they were halfway to the barn. "I know your mother is only teasing. It's obvious how much she loves you."

She realized her fingers were still wrapped around Cisco's muscular arm. She could feel the heat of his skin through his shirt and pulled away as if touching him for too long might actually burn her.

"Weren't you laying it on a little thick in there?" she asked as she stepped away.

"Your mother is a lovely woman." He lifted one finger and trailed it along her jaw. "You look like her, you know?"

How did he always throw her off balance? Delaney wanted a man in her life to hold her steady, but she couldn't deny the way Cisco made her feel.

"You're a lady-killer." She shook her head. "I can't tell if what you say to me is the truth or just another one of your well-rehearsed lines."

His thick brows drew together and a look of actual pain crossed his face before his practiced smile was in place once more. "You are beautiful, Delaney. That's the truth."

She didn't want to respond to him, didn't want to lean in as he brought his face closer to hers. Then the door to the barn slammed shut and Delaney jumped back. Just because Cisco had agreed to spend time on the ranch, it didn't change the fact that he was a big-city jet-setter. But change was inevitable. It was coming to Horseback Hollow and maybe she could change Cisco Mendoza, as well. Eventually Cisco had to fall for one woman and change his ways.

Delaney had no doubt she was strong enough to be that one.

Chapter Four

Cisco stretched his arms out in front of him as he walked toward the main gate at Cowboy Country several days later. For the first time since the barbecue, he hadn't gone to the ranch, needing a day to catch up on his work at Cowboy Country and unsure he could spend one more moment with Delaney Fortune Jones and keep his hands to himself.

She tempted him in a way no other woman had before, and Cisco had been with plenty of women in his life. But Delaney was different, smart and sexy but also sweet and innocent. She was totally confident in who she was and wouldn't let anyone steer her off course.

It was clear she was dedicated to the ranch and the values her parents had instilled in her and her siblings.

Cisco could relate to that as his father and mother had done the same thing for him and his brothers and sister.

That was part of the reason he was so conflicted when it came to Delaney. He hadn't exactly lied to her about his involvement in the luxury condos Cowboy Country had planned, but he'd definitely avoided giving any details of why he needed a Fortune for his business deal. Yet when she turned those cornflower-blue eyes on him, there wasn't anything he could deny her, including the truth.

His hope was that as she and her family got to know him, they'd trust his judgment and give the planned community a chance. But the more Cisco understood about life in Horseback Hollow, the more he could see the design of the Cowboy Country condos and real life in this quaint town wouldn't mesh. He figured it was up to him to bring the two closer in line. He had a lot riding on this deal, both his reputation and his own money. He wasn't about to give up on making it work.

He waved to the security guard near the front entrance who was tasked with making sure no one but employees accessed the park until the official opening. He could see people in theme park uniforms milling about near several rides and attractions and took a quick turn down a path that led to the corporate offices of Moore Entertainment. He knew there weren't many locals involved in the park at this point but didn't want to take the chance on someone in the park recognizing him. Until he had everything worked out, he wanted to keep his relationship with Cowboy Country under wraps.

He heard shouting as he came up the steps to the building. The door banged open and an older man stomped out, muttering to himself. "You're going to be sorry," he shouted over his shoulder. "Horses aren't mechanical. They're smart, strong, living animals and you need to treat them with the respect they deserve."

His angry gaze caught on Cisco and he shook his head. "Another suit," he all but spit. "Just what this place needs."

Cisco glanced down at himself. It was true that for his meeting with Kent Stephens this morning he'd traded his Western clothes for the more familiar feel of a tailored silk shirt and pressed trousers.

"What's the problem?" he asked.

The man hitched his thumb toward the corporate office. "The problem is that any real cowboy worth his salt knows he's only as good as the horseflesh he owns and how he treats his animals. Those fools wouldn't know how to take care of a barn full of horses if their lives depended on it." He shook his head. "They can find a new head trainer. I'm not putting myself on the line just so Alden Moore can make a fast buck."

Cisco wanted to question him further, but the guy took off down the steps and toward the front of the park. Pulling open the door, Cisco glanced at the young receptionist who stared back at him with wide eyes.

"Hello, Mr. Mendoza," she said calmly, her smile composed. "Mr. Stephens is expecting you."

He raised a brow at her placid expression and hitched his head toward the door. "Everything okay this morning, Janie?"

"No different than most days," she said in a softer tone. "I'm getting used to the sound of the door slamming."

Cisco used two fingers to massage his forehead. He'd heard rumors in town of employee unrest at Cowboy Country but hadn't wanted to believe they were true. If anything could kill a real estate deal before the financing was secured, it was dissension within the company.

These days, investors didn't want to promise their money if the business wasn't smooth and successful. There was too much at stake and too many other projects vying for the same pool of funds.

"You do a wonderful job at the front," he told the young woman. "Don't give up on things yet. It will all work out."

"Thanks, Mr. Mendoza." Her eyes turned soft as she leaned forward over her desk. "It's always a better day when you come to the office."

He smiled automatically and opened his mouth to offer her some flirtatious rejoinder, then stopped himself. Delaney's words about him being a lady-killer popped into his head. There was no doubt Cisco loved women, and flirting came as naturally as breathing to him. But now he held back, only nodding in response. He'd never given a second thought to how he'd come across before, but suddenly he wanted to save his banter for a tiny blonde cowgirl.

Before he could decide what that meant, Kent Stephens stuck his head out of the door to his office. "Mendoza, in here now. We need to talk."

Kent paced back and forth on the far side of his desk as Cisco entered. Although the building was cooled with central air, a fine sheen of sweat shone on the man's forehead as he talked into his cell phone. "I don't care. Send her out now." He hit a button and tossed his phone onto the desk. "I'm pulling more help from our other locations." He shook his head, running his hands through his hair, leaving it flopping over his wide forehead. "At this rate, Cowboy Country is going to be completely run by people from out of state. It's like no one in this godforsaken town needs a job."

"Who was the man leaving?"

"The guy we'd hired to manage the Wild West show. He's got decades of experience with horses but doesn't want to do things the way we expect."

"But wouldn't you defer to him as the expert?" Cisco asked, taking a seat in front of the desk.

"All we defer to is the bottom line." Kent dropped into the wide leather chair on the other side of the desk. "Everything Alden Moore touches turns to gold. Every park, every investment, each new idea. All of them have been a success until now."

"Cowboy Country hasn't even opened yet," Cisco argued. "You can't know it isn't going to be a success."

Kent pointed a finger at Cisco. "That's why I like you, Mendoza. You're confident. We need more of that attitude around here." His hand curled into a fist. "What we need less of is country-bumpkin locals stirring up trouble for us. Hasn't anyone in Horseback Hollow ever heard of progress?"

"I don't think it's progress they're against," Cisco answered carefully. "But there are traditions here—authentic cowboy traditions—and the people who value them don't want to feel like some big corporation is making a mockery of the life they hold dear."

"We're not making fun of anyone," Kent practically growled in response. "We just want to make some damn money." He shook his head. "Mr. Moore doesn't like the bad publicity. We need a shot in the arm to turn the tide of public sentiment in our favor." He stood and crossed his arms over his chest. "The condos could do it for us. They're a clean slate. No one has any preconceived notions, so if we handle the announcement right, it could help the whole operation. How's it coming with the Fortunes?"

"It's coming," Cisco answered. "I've been spending time with some of them and—"

"Priming the pump, right?" Kent looked hopeful.

Cisco inwardly cringed. "I wouldn't describe it that way." He could only imagine how Delaney would react if she heard Kent's words. "They're good people, Kent. But like most of the town, the Fortunes have concerns surrounding anything to do with Cowboy Country. I'm in the process of building relationships. These things take time."

"I don't care what you call it," Kent said quickly. "As long as you get them on board. You're our rainmaker, Cisco. Right now we could use a typhoon-level storm."

"I've got it under control." Cisco nodded. "I'm meeting with a group of investors down in Lubbock next week. Even if the Fortunes don't pan out, I'll get the backing for the condos."

"Whoa there." Kent held up his hands. "Other investors are fine, but we need you to pull in the Fortunes. The family has a ton of money, and they're going to put some of it into Cowboy Country. That was the deal when we hired you. Don't forget it."

"No chance of that with you reminding me every chance you get."

"Sorry. Like I said, we need some good news around here. It would go a long way toward solidifying your place with Moore Entertainment if you were the guy to bring it." He pushed a stack of papers forward on his desk. "Take a look at these. Moore Entertainment has a lot of plans once Cowboy Country is solid. This company has a bright future and there's a lot of opportunity for someone like you, Cisco. Don't blow it before you even get started."

At the moment, Cisco was more worried about how his involvement with the theme park was going to affect his relationship with Delaney once that news became public. In a very short time, she'd become an important part of his life. More important than he could remember a woman ever being for him.

But he had to keep his head on straight. He'd stayed in Horseback Hollow for business, and he didn't fail once he put his mind to something. He had too much at stake, both professionally and financially, to let this be the first time. He'd figure out how to handle Delaney and do this deal. He was certain he could make both things work.

He just had no idea how.

"You're really staying in Horseback Hollow for the long haul?" Cisco glanced at his brother as he parked his truck in front of the building that housed the Fortune Foundation.

"Absolutely," Matteo answered without hesitation. "This is where Rachel wants to be, so it works for me." He gave Cisco a light poke to the shoulder. "I'm not going to let her too far out of my sight and have some slick charmer like you try to put the moves on her again."

Cisco was relieved to see Matteo's grin as he said the words. "You two are a great match," he told his brother. "No other man would have a chance with her."

"What about you?"

"What about me?" Cisco paused before turning off the ignition.

"I'm surprised you've lasted here so long," Matteo said. "Aren't you missing some important shindigs this time of year in South Beach? I can't imagine how all the movers and shakers are surviving without you."

"I don't actually miss it that much," Cisco said, surprised the words were true. "The clubs and parties all run together after a while, you know?"

"I know," Matteo said, climbing out of the truck. "But I can't believe you're saying that. You don't have any big deals in the works? It's not like you, man."

"I have deals going," Cisco said. "You've heard of cell phones and the internet, right?"

"You're even looking more Texas than Miami." Matteo pointed to Cisco's boots. "That looks like genuine dirt on your heels."

"I've been helping out a little on the Fortune Jones ranch," Cisco answered evenly. He took a few more steps before realizing his brother had stopped. He turned to see Matteo practically doubled over, his shoulders shaking with laughter.

Matteo straightened and wiped a sleeve across his cheeks. "You mean to tell me you've become a ranch hand?" He shook his head. "I don't believe it. You're a city slicker through and through, Cisco. What gives?"

Cisco lifted his hands, frustrated at his brother's reaction. "I'm not a stranger to real work. Dad always had plenty of jobs for us around the house. I wanted to get to know the Fortunes a little better. Gabi's married into the family now and Dad works with them. I've got some time on my hands and this seemed like a good way to understand more about the Fortunes and the town itself. From what I understand, ranching is a big part of Horseback Hollow."

Matteo nodded. "It makes sense but I'm not sure I buy it." He held up his hand when Cisco would have argued.

"I'm not going to push you, bro. You do what you need to do. This is a great little community." He scrubbed a hand over his face. "I can't believe I'm saying this, but I'm happy to have a chance to spend some more time with you." He clapped Cisco on the back. "We've been at odds for too long."

"It's good to hang out with you, too, Matteo." Cisco hadn't realized how much the contentious relationship with his brother had hurt him until they'd begun to heal the rift between them. He paused at the entrance of the Fortune Foundation. "Are you sure it isn't going to be weird for Rachel to have me here with you?"

"We're solid," his brother assured him. "Even though she's with the right brother, she still likes you." Matteo rolled his eyes. "Cisco Mendoza and his legendary charm. It never fails."

For Cisco there was only one woman he was interested in charming these days. And when he stepped into the offices of the Horseback Hollow branch of the Fortune Foundation, he found himself looking right at her.

Delaney swallowed a gasp as Cisco walked into the Fortune Foundation office. She whipped her head around, afraid if she was caught looking at him, her gaze would give away her feelings.

"Hey there, sweetie," Rachel Robinson said from her place behind the reception desk.

Delaney's eyes widened and she turned again, relieved to see Cisco's brother Matteo follow him in.

"Hello, gorgeous." Matteo stepped up to the desk to give Rachel a short kiss.

Cisco continued to look at Delaney, one side of his mouth quirked.

"Hi, Delaney," Matteo said as he straightened.

"What...? Oh...hi, Matteo." She forced her gaze away from Cisco, then glanced back to him with a look she hoped was casual. "Hi, Cisco. What are you two doing here?"

"I came to take Rachel to lunch," Matteo told her. "Cisco tagged along. Suddenly he's interested in all things Fortune."

"Not all," Cisco clarified, his eyes on Delaney. "But I find some things about the Fortunes fascinating."

She felt Rachel and Matteo looking between the two of them. At that moment, the door swung open again and her brother Christopher walked through along with her sister, Stacey. Delaney bit her lip and tried to calm her rapidly beating heart. She'd never been able to hide anything from Stacey and worried her older sister would immediately guess at her growing feelings for Cisco. Feelings she wanted to both ignore and deny.

Cisco Mendoza wasn't good for her. He was the opposite of the type of man she needed in her life, but she couldn't stop thinking about him. Each day he came to the ranch to help seemed brighter and more exciting just because of his presence. He made her feel things she'd never imagined and she wanted more from him. She still wasn't ready to settle down and when she eventually did, she knew it would be with a man who was more like her. But she couldn't deny that she wanted to explore her reaction to Cisco, although not with two of her siblings looking on.

He'd met both Christopher and Stacey at her parents' recent barbecue, so everyone said hello and Stacey came over to give Delaney a hug.

"I feel like I haven't seen you forever," her sister

said. "Mom says you've been working extra hours on the ranch. Piper's been asking for Aunt Delaney. I tried calling you the other day. One of Colton's old friends is coming into town in a few weeks. I thought we could all go out to dinner."

"No way, Stacey." Delaney shrugged out of her sister's grasp. "I told you no matchmaking for me. I'm not settling down anytime soon and when I do, it will be on my own terms."

Stacey flicked a look at Christopher over her shoulder. "Tell your baby sister how great it feels to be in love."

"It's great," Christopher said with a smile.

"You're supposed to be on my side," Delaney protested, hands on her hips.

Christopher held up his hands. "I *am* on your side. I'm only telling you the truth, but you don't see me trying to set you up with any eligible bachelors."

"Because you don't know any," Stacey said.

"I know plenty," their brother countered. "In fact, we've got one right here. Cisco's an eligible bachelor. But I'm not pushing Delaney toward him. She'll find her own way, Stacey, when the time is right."

Matteo let out a laugh. "Cisco's the last man on earth you'd want to set up with your sister," he told the group. "Unless you want her courting trouble."

Delaney saw a muscle twitch in Cisco's jaw. "Thanks for the vote of confidence," he muttered, shaking his head.

"Just think about it," Stacey said to Delaney, ignoring the exchange between the Mendoza brothers. "Text me if you change your mind."

"I won't change my mind."

"Is your necklace new?" Stacey pointed to Delaney's throat. "I haven't seen you wear it before."

"I noticed it, too," Rachel added. "I love the charm."

Stacey nodded. "It's perfect for you. Where'd you get it? I hope you didn't take a trip to Vicker's Corners without me."

Delaney shook her head and flicked her gaze to Cisco. He was deep in conversation with Christopher and Matteo. She brought her fingers to her throat, touching the outline of the state of Texas. "I picked it up when I was out one day with Mom," she lied. "I don't remember where, but I've had it for a while."

"If you think about where it came from, let me know," Stacey told her. "I've got to get back home." She gave Delaney another hug. "I really want you to go to dinner with us. No pressure, just a fun night out."

Stacey said goodbye to everyone else and walked out.

"Are you okay if I head out to lunch?" Rachel asked Christopher. "Kinsley should be back soon."

"I can hold down the fort." Delaney watched as Christopher turned to Cisco. "Give me a call if you want to get more involved like we discussed at the barbecue. There's a lot to be done in this community and we can use all the help we can get. In fact, if you have a few minutes now, I can give you more details about the elementary school project I mentioned."

"Sure." He turned to Matteo. "I'll see you tomorrow for breakfast with Dad and Gabi?"

Matteo nodded, wrapping his arm around Rachel's shoulder. "I'll be there."

"Good to see you, Rachel." Cisco nodded at the other woman. Delaney studied him as he said the words, trying to decide if there was any lingering regret or sadness over the girl he'd loved and lost. But if Cisco harbored any feelings for Rachel, he kept them hidden.

"Delaney, do you want to join us for lunch?" Rachel asked kindly.

Delaney shook her head, having no desire to be the third wheel on Matteo and Rachel's lunch date. "I have a few things to take care of in town. I'll give you a call later this week about getting together."

Rachel smiled. "I'd like that."

As Matteo and Rachel left, Christopher wrapped her in a bear hug, lifting her off her feet. "Don't let Stacey get to you, Flapjack. She thinks now that the rest of us have found love, you and Galen need to fall in line."

"I don't fall in line for anyone," Delaney answered, squirming out of his grasp.

"Did you call her Flapjack?" Cisco raised his brows. "Like her horse?"

Christopher looked between Cisco and Delaney. "How do you know she has a horse named Flapjack?" Suddenly he was her overprotective big brother again.

"He's been helping Dad at the ranch," Delaney said quickly.

Christopher's shrewd gaze narrowed. "You don't seem like the cowboy type."

"That's why I wanted to get some experience, to see what real life is like in Horseback Hollow." Cisco gave Christopher an easy smile. "I have a lot of respect for your father and the operation he's built."

"He's got a damn strong work ethic," Christopher agreed. "So does this one." He ruffled Delaney's hair, and she rolled her eyes in response. "It's true. What you lack in size you make up for in spunk."

He flashed Cisco a grin. "She has an appetite to match.

That's how she got the nickname Flapjack. She could eat more of our mother's pancakes than any of the boys even when she could barely see over the table. Her horse has an appetite just as big, so we started calling him Flapjack in her honor. The name stuck."

Cisco nodded, looking like he was trying to hold back a laugh. "That's cute."

Cute and spunky. Delaney gave a mental groan. She'd never minded being described as cute or spunky until she met Cisco. But she knew his type was long legged and sophisticated, like Rachel Robinson. He'd never be truly interested in someone like Delaney and the knowledge grated on her nerves.

"I've got to go." She chucked her brother on the shoulder. "Thanks for having my back with Stacey. I know she means well but everywhere I turn, a sibling wants to set me up with a friend. I can handle my own life, you know?"

"I know." Christopher's smile was gentle. "I felt the same way."

Cisco took a step forward. "Actually, I forgot something I need to take care of this afternoon. Christopher, is it okay if I text you later this week to set up a meeting?"

"Sure thing," her brother answered. His cell phone rang and he glanced down. "This is a call I've been expecting. I'll talk to you both later."

Delaney didn't wait for Cisco. She pushed her way out into the bright afternoon sunlight. The heels of her boots clicked on the sidewalk as she walked toward the truck she'd parked two blocks down. But within a few steps, Cisco's long-legged strides matched hers.

"I don't need an escort," she told him, flipping her

sunglasses onto the bridge of her nose. "You told Christopher you need to take care of something. Go for it."

"Slow down, Flapjack."

"Don't call me that." Delaney whirled around, pointing her finger at Cisco. "I can't stand it when my brothers use that name. There's no way I'm letting you get away with it."

"Sorry," Cisco said with a slow wink. "I think it's cute."

Delaney stomped her foot, actually stomped her boot on the sidewalk. "Cute," she spit out. "Next you're going to add *spunky*."

"Well…" Cisco flashed a smile. He pointed the toe of his boot toward hers. "Now that you mention it."

"Don't you dare." Delaney jabbed her finger into his chest, growing frustrated when he didn't move an inch. She'd been admiring all that lean muscle for the past week, but now his strength only fueled her anger.

"Have dinner with me," Cisco said gently, wrapping his own fingers around hers.

The invitation should have thrilled her, but she was too irritated to appreciate it. She didn't want to be one of the legions of Cisco Mendoza fans.

"No."

He chuckled. "Come on, Delaney. You know you want to go out with me."

Chapter Five

Delaney spun around, walking away. Never in his life had a woman turned her back on him. Cisco found her willingness to leave him in the dust made him want her all the more. Delaney was more than a distraction. He cared for her and right now he couldn't stand the idea that he'd somehow, even if inadvertently, hurt her. By the time he truly registered the meaning of that, she was halfway down the block.

Cisco ran to catch up, reaching her just as she was stepping off the curb to cross the street. "Delaney, wait." He reached for her but stopped when she slapped at his hand, not breaking her stride. "I'm sorry," he told her.

At that she stopped and turned to him. "Sorry for what?" The way her eyes narrowed gave him pause.

Cisco was pretty sure this was a test, one he couldn't afford to fail. There was no doubt he had a line for every occasion. He'd been cultivating the gift of sweet-talking women since he'd first noticed girls. But when he answered Delaney's question, he tried a new tactic—the truth.

"I'm sorry I hurt you. I care about you, Delaney. Please have dinner with me."

"So you can learn more about the Fortunes?"

"I want to learn more about *you*."

She studied him for a long moment. "Where would you take me?"

"My place. Let me cook for you."

"*You* cook?"

"I've been known to occasionally." He flashed her a smile, rewarded when one side of her mouth quirked. "Please, Delaney. It's obvious you don't want people to know we've been spending time together. I heard what you told your sister when she asked about the necklace." Now he couldn't resist. With the tip of one finger, he traced the delicate gold at her throat.

Her breath hitched in response and her blue eyes darkened, but her gaze didn't waver from his. He loved her bravery.

"I don't want anyone to get the wrong idea about us," she told him, her voice a whisper.

"What's the wrong idea?"

"That this is anything more than you meeting my conditions in order to help you with a business deal."

"What if I want it to be more?" He lifted his hand from her neck and tucked a stray piece of hair behind her ear.

She shook her head. "We have a temporary arrangement, Cisco. That's all it is."

He didn't believe she meant those words. He wanted to pull her into his arms and prove how wrong she was. To show her what she meant to him. But Delaney deserved more—she deserved to be treasured and cherished. For once in his life, Cisco was going to be the man who did the right thing. The thought that the best thing he could do was tell her the entire truth of the situation niggled in the back of his mind, but he pushed it away.

"Will you come to dinner?" he asked again. "Please."

She squeezed shut her eyes as if debating with herself. "Fine," she answered after a moment, opening them again. "Tomorrow night."

"Whenever you want," he agreed.

"Do you ever not get your way?" She sounded irritated but a trace of a smile played at the corner of her lips.

"Not if I can help it." He bent forward and dropped a quick kiss on the tip of her nose. "I'll see you tomorrow, Delaney."

Delaney heard voices as she came down the steps in her parents' house and saw Stacey's car in the driveway. "I'm taking off, Mom," she called, heading for the front door. "I won't be late." The last thing Delaney wanted was to be grilled by her sister tonight.

"Where are you going looking so nice?"

Her sister walked out from the kitchen along with their mother. Delaney smoothed a hand over the pale blue sundress that grazed her knees. It was one of her favorites and tonight she'd paired it with cream-colored cowboy boots and beaded earrings she'd borrowed from her mother.

"She has a date," Jeanne Marie said with a smile.

"A date with who?" Stacey asked the same time Delaney said, "It's not a date, Mom."

"Cisco Mendoza," her mother answered. "He's been

working at the ranch for the past couple of weeks. He and your sister have grown close."

"We're friends," Delaney insisted, feeling color rise to her cheeks.

"I knew it," Stacey said, flashing a triumphant smile. "I knew something was going on when I saw the two of you at Christopher's office."

"Nothing is going on," Delaney insisted. "He's new to town and doesn't know a lot of people."

Stacey laughed. "Somehow I don't think Cisco would have a problem finding companionship, especially of the female variety."

"He cares about your sister," Jeanne Marie said, wrapping her arm around Stacey's waist. "It's sweet the way he looks at her."

"Sweet," Stacey repeated, her smile widening.

"It's only dinner." Delaney grabbed her purse from the hall table, then turned to her mother. "How does he look at me?"

"Like you are precious to him."

Delaney's hand stilled as she met her mother's knowing gaze. Even Stacey fell quiet. That was exactly how Delaney wanted Cisco to look at her. The fact that her mother believed it to be true gave her a boost in confidence that made her anticipate this night in an entirely different way.

"I won't be late," she said, her voice shaking the tiniest bit.

"Wait a second," Stacey said before she turned and disappeared into the kitchen.

Jeanne Marie stepped toward Delaney when it was just the two of them. "You *are* precious, sweetie. My greatest wish is that you have someone in your life who makes you feel that every day. I've wished that for all of my children."

Stacey returned, digging through her purse as she walked. "Here, take this." She held out a tube of lip gloss to Delaney. "I got a new color last week. It'll look great on you."

Suddenly Delaney was transported back to high school, sharing secrets, makeup and a bathroom with her sister as they got ready on a Friday night. It reminded her of how lucky she was to be a part of this family, to be surrounded by so many people who loved her—even if their brand of love could feel smothering at times. They only wanted what was best for her.

For what seemed like the millionth time in the past several days, Delaney wondered if Cisco could be it.

She hugged her mother and Stacey, then headed to her truck. Her parents' ranch was several miles outside of town, so it took her about twenty minutes to make it to the address Cisco had texted her earlier. Delaney parked at the curb of the small house he'd rented near downtown.

The door opened just as she reached the top step of the porch. Cisco greeted her with a wide smile. "You look beautiful as always," he told her, his gaze warming her from head to toe.

Even though she knew it was probably just another one of his well-practiced lines, the deep tone of his voice made Delaney shiver. He took a step back to allow her through the door, but she paused. She felt suddenly shy, as if this night was going to change something big in her life.

Cisco didn't say anything. He stood watching her, waiting for her to choose. Doubt flickered in his eyes, only for a moment, but it made all the difference to her.

Because that trace of vulnerability, the chink in his worldly armor, made her know that she wasn't alone in her feelings. Cisco was as affected by whatever was going on between them as she was, and for all his confidence, he didn't know quite how to handle her.

She had to believe she was more than just another conquest for him, that she was special. She took a step forward and his gaze softened. Her breath caught in her throat. Her mother was right. He looked at her as if she was precious. Even if what they had was temporary, Delaney wanted to revel in the way he made her feel. She wanted to be precious to him.

"You look pretty good yourself, Mr. Mendoza," she said as she came toward him. Tonight he wore a dark gray shirt rolled to his elbows with jeans and his cowboy boots. His Miami style was melding with the Western influence of Horseback Hollow and the results made her stomach dance with desire.

He took her hand in his and lifted it, grazing his mouth across her knuckles. "I hope you're hungry," he whispered, his dark eyes intense.

A mix of nerves and excitement had Delaney bursting out with laughter. "You can save the lines for another girl, Cisco. I don't need them."

He shook his head, but instead of being irritated at her rebuff, he gave her a genuine smile. "That hurts." He nipped at the tips of her fingers before releasing her hand. "You, Delaney Fortune Jones, are the worst thing that's happened to my ego in years."

Looking at Cisco, all masculine swagger wrapped up in a delicious package, she couldn't imagine anything wounding him. "I'm sure your ego will survive."

She wondered if the same could be said for her heart.

"Please come all the way in, *mi cielo*. I *do* hope you're hungry." He followed her into the house, leaning forward over her shoulder. "Although to hear your brother tell it, you always have an appetite."

"My brother exaggerates. Sort of."

Cisco laughed again and Delaney relaxed. As much as she found her physical attraction to him unsettling, Delaney simply liked being around Cisco. He made her smile, made her feel intelligent and interesting. But his true motives were still a bit of a mystery, and she wanted to know more about him. Her gaze traveled around the house to see if the interior gave her any clues to the man. Something smelled wonderful, rich and spicy, and she automatically headed toward the kitchen.

"This place is nice," she said as she walked through an open living room.

Cisco shrugged. "It came furnished, which is fine since my stay in Horseback Hollow is temporary. I had a few things flown in from Miami to make it more comfortable while I'm here."

Light spilled into the homey kitchen. A cherry-patterned wallpaper covered the walls and lace curtains hung on either side of a window in the breakfast nook. The kitchen table was made of oak, solid and a little worn. The cabinets were a faded cream color with colorful tiles on the counters.

It was what filled the counters that made her stop in her tracks. "Is this a kitchen or a science lab?"

She turned to Cisco, who'd come to stand next to her looking genuinely confused. "What do you mean?"

She walked to the far counter, tracing her fingers across the stainless steel machines situated in a neat row along the wall. "All of this stuff." She pointed to a huge steel contraception with more control buttons than her truck had. "What in the world is that used for?"

"It's a coffeemaker."

"We have a coffeemaker at the ranch. That looks more like a flight simulator."

"I told you," he said, moving to the stove to stir something in a large pot. "I had some things flown in from Miami. A good cup of coffee is important in the morning."

"Did you work at Starbucks in a past life?" she wondered out loud.

He chuckled. "Would you like a glass of wine?"

"Sure, thanks." She couldn't take her eyes off the upscale appliances. There was an industrial-size blender and another machine she didn't even recognize.

"It's a juicer," Cisco told her as he took a pitcher from the refrigerator.

"Right." Some of her doubts about this evening returned. She was a simple cowgirl, a native Texan and proud of it. Yes, she liked Cisco. She was attracted to him. But could it be anything more than that? He was sophisticated and used to the finer things in life. Delaney had no use for fancy frills. Family, friends, her horse and some good food made her happy. She had no intention of changing who she was but worried that at the end of the day, she wouldn't be enough for a man like Cisco.

"Stop." His voice broke through her musings. He was next to her at the counter, standing so close she could see the shadow of stubble on his jaw. He handed her a glass but linked his fingers with hers for a moment when she took it from him. "They're appliances, Delaney. They don't mean anything."

She wasn't certain she agreed. "Your wine has fruit in it."

He nodded. "It's actually sangria. It's my mother's recipe. She made it on special occasions. Gabi, my brothers and I loved to watch the fruit soak, although we were never allowed a sip." He shrugged his shoulders, suddenly looking unsure. "Actually, everything tonight is food my mom loved. I don't normally cook family recipes for…well, for anyone outside the family. But I thought you'd like it."

She took a sip of the dark pink drink. "The sangria is a good start."

"Wait until you try the picadillo. I've adjusted it a bit from my mom's recipe to give it a more Cuban flavor. Food is a big perk about living in Miami. There are so many ethnicities in the city and the food reflects that mix."

Delaney swallowed a bit nervously. She wasn't usually adventurous with food. Her idea of a perfect meal was the grilled cheese sandwich at the Horseback Hollow Grill, but she wasn't about to admit that to Cisco.

"What can I do to help?" she asked, looking around the kitchen.

"You can stand there and look gorgeous."

She shook her head. "I'm not exactly the stand-around type."

"Really?" He quirked a brow. "I hadn't noticed."

She scrunched up her nose. "Let me help."

"If you'd like, you can set the table. There are plates and silverware ready to go on the edge of the counter."

"Lucky for you I have years of experience with table setting."

She put out the plates, forks and knives, then found napkins in a lower drawer.

By the time she was finished, Cisco was bringing a large bowl of rice and another with a savory mix of meat, peppers and onions all in a tomato-based sauce. She had to admit it looked and smelled amazing.

He pulled out a chair and she sat, spreading her napkin across her lap.

Before joining her, he took a lighter out of a drawer and lit two candles in the middle of the table.

"Nice touch," she told him.

He sat across from her and lifted his glass. "To new friends and new adventures."

Their glasses clinked and Delaney didn't bother to hide her smile. She was ready for a new adventure with Cisco Mendoza.

Chapter Six

Cisco realized he was holding his breath as he watched Delaney take her first bite of the meal. He rarely cooked at home anymore. Most of the women he dated expected to be wined and dined, always wanting a table at the hottest new restaurant in Miami. Cisco had never minded. Part of his job was to be seen by investors as a power player and securing an unattainable reservation added to his status.

For Delaney he wanted something different. He wanted to show her who he truly was, not the mask he'd created for his public persona. He was proud to be the son of Orlando and Luz Mendoza and happy that, for once, his character seemed to matter more than his reputation.

Her eyes drifted shut as she chewed and he leaned forward, trying to gauge her reaction. After a moment her eyes popped open again. "This is amazing." She looked from her plate to him. "You really made this?"

"No, I had it flown in from South Beach."

When her face started to fall, he laughed. "I'm joking, Delaney. Of course I made it."

"Your cousin could serve this at the Cantina. It's that good."

He took a bite himself. "I'm glad you think so, although I don't think Marcus and Wendy need any help from me."

"Tell me about the dish."

"It's nothing fancy," he said, a little embarrassed at the attention she was paying to the food. Which was strange because Cisco generally liked attention of any kind. "You take ground beef, onion, garlic, peppers, olives and raisins, then—"

"Olives?" Delaney asked, poking her fork at the dish. "Don't tell my mom I ate olives. They're on my no-eat list."

"You have a list of foods you don't eat?"

She shrugged. "Mainly just olives. And artichokes."

"I'm going to make you love artichokes," he told her.

A tiny voice inside his head whispered, *More important, make her love you.* He wasn't sure where that thought came from. Cisco wasn't looking for love. Sure, he was attracted to Delaney and he liked spending time with her. But love? Cisco wasn't ready for love. Or was he?

"I'd never guess olives and raisins could coexist. What comes next?" She continued eating.

Cisco shook his head to clear it, then answered, "I sauté the meat and onions, then add the other vegetables. Pour in tomato sauce and the spices and simmer for several hours. It's really simple, actually. The spice mix is the most important part. My mother also had a special way of making rice. Her secret was soaking the uncooked rice in water before adding it to the pot. It cooks up better. No matter where my dad's career took us in the world, my mom always made her signature dishes when we first moved to make sure wherever we were felt like home."

She took a bite of salad dressed with a tangy vinaigrette, then pulled off a nibble of crusty bread. "The whole meal is excellent," Delaney told him. "You still miss your mom. I can tell."

Cisco shifted in his chair. He was a private man and didn't usually discuss things as close to his heart as his mother. But Delaney had managed to move past the walls he'd erected and he wanted her to understand what this night meant to him. "She was the heart and soul of our family. Her death took a toll on all of us, especially my father. They had a true love story, and it was difficult to see him without her. We kind of went our separate ways after she passed. That's one of the reasons it's been good to spend time in Horseback Hollow since my dad, Gabi and Matteo are here. Family is important."

"It is," Delaney agreed. "I'm glad you've stayed here."

The shy smile she gave him made his heart squeeze. "Me, too."

"How are the plans going for your meeting?"

"Meeting?" he repeated, blinking.

"The reason you need a Fortune. The whole purpose of you spending time with me."

He couldn't believe he'd all but forgotten about his initial reason for seeking out Delaney Fortune Jones. He knew better than to let his emotions distract him from business. He'd worked long and hard to become successful. Was he really going to let that go so easily? Still, it irritated him to think that Delaney might doubt his feelings for her. "Do you really believe that's the reason we're together tonight?"

She met his gaze across the table. "I don't know, Cisco. I hope it's not, but I honestly don't know."

"My business in Horseback Hollow is on track, although still in the planning stages."

"Which means you aren't going to give me any details."

"Not yet. But I want you to know you mean more to me than only someone who can help further a deal. I've been focused on my career for a long time, and I'm proud of what I've accomplished. I expect success because I work hard for it. But I want to work at this, too." He motioned between the two of them. "Give me a chance to show you that my intentions are honorable, Delaney. I want to…court you."

"Court me?" She tilted her head as if mulling over the words. "That seems like a pretty old-fashioned concept for a guy who needs a bunch of bells and whistles just to make a cup of coffee."

"There's a time for modern luxury and a place for time-honored customs." He hit a few buttons on his iPhone and pushed back from the table, holding out his hand to her. Music began to play from the portable speakers he'd installed around the house. "May I have this dance, Ms. Fortune?"

Delaney wanted nothing more than to rush into his arms, but something held her back. There were a lot of things in life Delaney knew she could do well. Dancing wasn't one of them. It's what had made her run away from him at Jude and Gabi's reception. She had no intention of running now, but still…

She hopped to her feet and lifted her plate and one of the serving bowls off the table. "We should clean up the dishes."

Cisco drew back his hand, watching her with a curious look in his eye. "You don't like salsa music?"

"It's not that, although I'm more a straight-up country girl. Give me some Kenny Chesney or Carrie Underwood and I'm happy."

Cisco groaned. "*Mi cielo*, tonight you put the arrow straight through my heart." He pretended to stagger toward the counter, setting down his dishes when he got there. "This music feels like home to me. It gets into your soul, Delaney. Tell me you don't feel the rhythm." He swayed back and forth to the music, his arms in a wide circle as if he were already holding her tight.

Of course he was a fantastic dancer. Delaney figured there was nothing related to wooing a woman that Cisco hadn't mastered. The thought made her stomach plunge as if it were on one of the rides being built at Cowboy Country.

She spun around and flipped on the water at the sink, her fingers trembling slightly as she rinsed off the plate. "I can't dance," she muttered, her back to Cisco.

"What was that?" He leaned in next to her and she was caught up in the subtle scent of his cologne. With one hand he tipped up her chin, while he turned off the water with the other. "What has you so bothered right now?"

"I can't dance," she said more forcefully, shaking her head. "I have two left feet, no rhythm, the whole bit." She set the plate in the sink, reaching around him to grab a towel. "The music is great. I love the beat." She took a step back. "Look, I can tap my toe." He glanced down to her booted foot as she tapped it on the kitchen floor.

"But that's it. Anything more and I'm lost. I don't two-step or line-dance, so you can bet I wouldn't be good at salsa dancing."

"You just haven't had the right partner."

"A partner who enjoys having his feet smashed?" She moved past him to the kitchen table. Before she could pick up another dish, he came to stand in front of her.

"Give it a chance, Delaney." He pocketed his phone, then took her hands. "One song."

His words echoed in her head. Something in the way he looked at her made her believe he was really asking her to give him a chance. "One song," she agreed reluctantly, then took a step toward him, feeling her body go rigid with nerves. "I hope your toes are ready for a beating."

Instead of taking her in his arms, he led her out of the kitchen toward the sliding door at the back of the house. "Where are we going?"

"Salsa is more than music—it's an experience to savor with your senses." He pulled out his phone and pressed another button as they stepped onto the back patio. The house was in a neighborhood but backed up to an open field, giving the yard a sense of privacy. Music began playing from a speaker mounted under the covered porch.

"You've got a heck of a stereo system for temporary housing," she said with a nervous laugh.

"I love music," he said simply. "The way it makes me feel. It can be relaxing or invigorating. The right beat sets the mood for an entire evening."

Delaney swallowed and gave a short nod. She wasn't used to being so far out of her element. Horseback Hollow was the only home she knew, every inch of the town familiar. But tonight felt as if she was in a brand-new world, a world where she wasn't in control.

"So now we dance?" she asked, trying and failing to make herself relax. The night had begun to cool and a gentle breeze moved through the air, tickling her bare arms. A mix of soft pink and purple colors streaked the sky and the clouds that floated above them took on a golden light. This was normally her favorite time of night, when the day quieted and she finished up her work in the gentle silence. But with Cisco standing in front of her she felt anything but relaxed and had to force herself not to run away in order to gain sway over her rioting emotions.

"Close your eyes."

She bit down on her lip but followed his request.

"Listen to the music," he said softly. "Feel the beat of it. Let the sound wash over you."

She tried to concentrate but he'd come closer to her and she could feel the heat from his body as he spoke. The music flowed through her at the same time Cisco's voice did crazy things to her insides.

"Why do you call me *mi cielo*?" she asked on a whisper of breath. "That translates to *my sky*. What does that mean?"

"That's the literal translation, yes," he answered, running one fingertip down her arm before lacing his hand in hers. "It is also a Spanish term of endearment. It can mean *my heaven*. That's how you feel to me, Delaney. Like heaven."

Delaney's eyes popped open. "Oh," was all she could manage.

"Are you ready?" His gaze was intense and tender at the same time.

As he looked at her, all her fears melted away. She lifted her free hand to his shoulder and he pulled her close. Delaney had always found being petite was a disadvantage to dancing, but Cisco had been correct about her needing the right partner. She fit perfectly against him.

He moved as she knew he would, a mix of easy grace and passionate spirit. She felt wild in his arms. His mouth grazed her ear as he hummed along with the melody. Delaney forgot her awkwardness and nerves. She became only movement and senses. Cisco's enticing scent mixed with the clean fragrance of the land made her feel intoxicated. His expertise in leading her through the steps of the dance gave her confidence and she moved her hips in time with a rhythm that seemed to come from a place deep inside her.

The song ended and a slower tune began to play. Cisco held her closer, wrapping his arm tightly around her back, his hand splayed across her hip. Delaney nuzzled into the crook of his neck, breathing him in as she felt his heart beating against her chest. Longing pooled inside her, a deep and restless desire she couldn't name and barely understood.

When he leaned back to look at her, she saw the same passion reflected in his eyes. "You are a beautiful dancer, *cielo.*"

"You are heaven." She whispered the translation and his gaze dropped to her mouth, darkening even more.

"Tonight there is nothing but this moment." He touched his lips to hers, gently exploring as if afraid she'd bolt if he was too aggressive.

But Delaney didn't want gentle. Being in Cisco's arms freed something reckless in her. She wanted everything he had to give and wound her arms around his neck, opening her mouth to deepen the kiss.

Chapter Seven

Cisco heard a moan and wasn't sure if it came from him or the woman wrapped around him. Delaney had been so responsive as they danced he couldn't resist kissing her. He was tired of fighting his growing feelings for her. He wanted her with a passion he'd never before experienced.

But he also respected her, and the secrets between them weighed heavily on his heart and conscience. So he'd kept the kiss gentle, allowing her time to become accustomed to his desire. As usual, she'd surprised him, taking control of the kiss with an innocent need that made his desire burst into flame.

He stroked his hands up and down her back, loving the feel of her compact curves. His tongue met hers, and they explored each other as the slow salsa rhythm played in the background. Cisco lost track of everything except Delaney, the flowery smell of her perfume and how soft and warm she felt in his arms. His fingers grazed the hem of her dress, lifting it, her skin like silk under his hands. He wanted her more than he'd wanted a woman in as long as he could remember.

Then, as suddenly as the kiss had started, Delaney pulled away. She took two steps back, her fingers covering her mouth, looking as dazed as he felt.

"That," she whispered, "was nice."

"Nice," he repeated, working to get his body under control.

She nodded. "Thank you."

He was having a hard time keeping up with her, especially since most of his blood flow seemed concentrated below his waist at the moment. "Why are you thanking me?"

Her hand fluttered in the air in front of her. The evening light had grown dim as they'd danced, so now her face was partially hidden in shadow. He could almost feel her pulling away from him and couldn't figure out what had gone wrong. "Dinner, the dancing, pretty much the whole night." She pulled her hand in tight to her stomach, as if it might flit away if she didn't hold it in place.

Cisco ran his own hand across his face. "What's wrong, Delaney?"

"Nothing," she answered quickly. "But I...you know... I promised my mom I wouldn't be late, so I should probably get going. Unless you want me to help with the dishes first." She glanced at the house over her shoulder. "I should help you finish cleaning the kitchen."

"I'll take care of the dishes." He took a step toward her, then stopped as she jumped back. She was spooked, no doubt about it. "I'll walk you to your car," he said gently, not wanting to push her for fear she might actually run away. This was something new, as well, a woman who wasn't throwing herself at him. Maybe that was what made his blood heat so quickly in response to her. Whatever it was, he didn't want to take a chance at messing it up.

She gave a curt nod. "I just need to grab my purse from inside."

He followed her into the house. She was moving as though her life depended on getting away from him quickly. He hated that, wanted to find a way to reassure her. He wanted to pull her into his arms again and make her never want to leave.

But he held back. He didn't touch her as she walked to her truck. She turned to him at the edge of the driveway. "Thank you," she said again, her eyes not meeting his.

"Thank you for joining me."

She glanced up at him from under her lashes as if she expected something more.

"It was a perfect evening," he told her, reaching forward slowly to take her hand in his. Her fingers remained stiff and he turned her hand and placed a soft kiss at the center of her palm. She gave a tiny gasp as if his mouth burned and he released her.

She nodded and whispered, "Thank you again," then scurried around the front of her truck, the interior light blinking on as she climbed in, illuminating her for just a second. Cisco could have sworn he saw a tear streak down her cheek.

Damn, what had gone wrong? He hated the thought that he'd made her cry for any reason, but especially one he didn't understand. His feelings for Delaney were a jumble in his mind, but he knew he wanted to be the man to put a smile on her face. He kicked his boot into the concrete and swore under his breath. Stepping out into the street, he watched the red glow of her truck's taillights disappear as she took the turn out of his neighborhood.

He couldn't remember the last time he'd been so frustrated. If her body's reaction was any indication, Delaney had been as affected by the kiss as him. He made his way slowly into the house, turned off the music and finished cleaning the kitchen. As he did, he thought about what he wanted from life. Things had always been clear for Cisco—success meant money, power and respect. He'd achieved all of those things but something had been missing, and until he'd come to Horseback Hollow, he hadn't realized what it was. He still couldn't put a name on it, but he knew it had something to do with the woman turning him inside out these past few weeks. He still had no doubt he could make things work out to his liking, including his relationship with Delaney.

The trick was figuring out how.

Delaney sat at the table in her parents' kitchen two days later, struggling to find the energy to start her day.

"Are you going to eat the eggs," her mother asked gently, "or make them into art on your plate?"

She set down her fork and pushed the plate to the side. "I'm sorry. I don't seem to have much of an appetite this morning."

"It happens, sweetie." Jeanne Marie eased into the chair next to Delaney and took her hand.

The small gesture made tears prick at the back of Delaney's eyes. "Oh, Mama, I messed up so badly."

Her mother's smile was gentle. "Tell me what happened."

"I didn't mean to like him so much." Delaney wiped the back of her plaid shirtsleeve across her cheek.

"I assume you're talking about Cisco?" her mother asked, taking a folded tissue out of the pocket of her soft denim blouse and handing it to Delaney.

"I just wanted to have some fun. You were right—I've been at loose ends now that everyone except Galen and me has paired off. I don't need to be in a serious relationship. That's not what I'm looking for and certainly not with a guy like Cisco."

"And what does that mean, 'a guy like Cisco'?"

Delaney sighed. "He's got all the right moves, you know? He's polished and smooth. I bet you he could charm any woman he meets. It's all an act and I wasn't going to fall for it. I know better."

"That's funny because he's seemed genuine in his attentions toward you."

"Don't you see?" Delaney asked, slapping her palm against the table. "That's what he does. He makes you feel—he made me feel—like someone special. Like I was different. Now I'm just another one of the endless parade of women who have fallen for his charms. I was going to keep my heart out of the mix, Mama. Give him a taste of his own medicine. I don't know why but I wanted to prove that I was immune to a man like Cisco. I've always wanted to be with someone like me, down-to-earth, simple. I don't need much to make me happy, but now I'm so confused."

"Oh, sweetie, I'm sorry."

"I wanted a man who would keep me steady and Cisco shakes my world to its foundation."

Her mother's brows drew together and suddenly Jeanne Marie looked more like a ferocious mama grizzly bear than the nurturing soul Delaney knew so well.

"Did he do something to hurt you, Delaney? Did he take advantage? Or say he didn't want to see you again?"

Delaney shifted in her chair, balling up the tissue her mother had given her. "Not exactly." She darted a glance at her mother, then back to the table. "He kissed me," she whispered.

"You didn't want him to?" Jeanne Marie asked softly.

"Oh, I wanted him to." She shook her head. "In fact, I kissed him back like my life depended on it. I've never had a reaction like that to a guy. It's so embarrassing. He made me feel...things I don't understand." She dropped the tissue on the table and covered her face in her hands. "Then I left. I freaked out and ran away. He probably thinks I'm a lunatic or the most pathetic girl he's ever met."

"I doubt that." Her mother gently peeled away Delaney's fingers. "Strong emotions can be difficult to manage at first. I'm sure Cisco understands that."

"But I haven't talked to him since then. I'm sure he wants nothing to do with me." Delaney hated that her voice sounded like a whine.

"Didn't you tell me he'd texted yesterday to say he had a meeting in Lubbock?"

"Yes, but I bet that was a big fat lie."

"Delaney, now you're being silly."

"I'm not, Mama. I don't see him showing up today. Chances are he's having a good laugh over the little Fortune Jones girl who got all twitterpated over him."

"Twitterpated," Jeanne Marie repeated with a chuckle. "That's how your grandma used to describe my feelings for your dad."

"But Dad felt the same way about you. It's different. Cisco isn't like that."

As if on cue, the sound of an engine rumbled up the driveway. From where she sat, Delaney looked out the kitchen window as a black truck parked near the barn.

Jeanne Marie lifted an eyebrow. "Are you expecting a visitor?"

Delaney jumped up from the table, smoothing her hands over her shirt. "It's him. He's here."

"I'm not surprised," her mother said simply.

Delaney darted toward the door, then turned back and gave her mom a quick hug. "I love you, Mama."

"You, too, sweetheart," Jeanne Marie answered.

Delaney reached for her plate but her mother waved her away. "I'll take care of things in here. You go on, now."

"You're the best," Delaney said, breaking into a wide grin. She tried to school her features as she walked out into the bright morning sunlight. Today was going to be a hot one, with the temperature already climbing.

Cisco turned as the door to the house shut. His mouth widened into a grin as he caught sight of her. This morning he wore a pair of dark jeans with a subtle Western shirt and his cowboy hat perched on the top of his head. He looked so handsome and so happy to see her that Delaney forgot her inner deal with herself to play things cool and collected.

Instead she bolted toward him, throwing her arms around his neck as her legs wrapped around his waist. She squeezed him as tight as she could, loving the feel of his warmth underneath her and the clean scent of him winding through her senses. He held her up as she clung to him, her face turning hot as she realized that she'd once again made a fool of herself in front of this man.

"I could get used to a greeting like that," he said with

a soft chuckle. She tried to unwind from him but he held her fast, giving her braid a gentle tug until she leaned back enough for him to look her in the eyes. "Good morning." He kissed her mouth, just a brush of his lips, then rested his forehead against hers. "I've missed you."

"Really? Even after how the other night ended?"

"Really." His fingers found the space between her shirt and jeans, their warmth on her bare skin making her tingle. "But I'm going to put you down before your father sees us and comes after me with a shotgun."

"He wouldn't do that," Delaney said with a laugh before untangling from Cisco's embrace.

He let her go but kept his hands on her waist, tracing small circles on her skin. "I had a great time when you came for dinner, Delaney. I'm sorry if I caught you off guard or moved too fast."

She shook her head. "You didn't. This is going to sound silly but I just haven't felt…" She trailed off, not sure how much she wanted to reveal.

Cisco bent his head, kissing her again. "I haven't felt this way, either."

She looked into his melted-chocolate eyes and saw that he was both sincere and unsure, something she hadn't expected from him.

"I brought you something," he told her, stepping back and leaning into his truck. He handed her a stainless steel travel mug. "The best coffee you'll ever have."

"Made with the most complicated coffeemaker I've ever seen."

She took a sip. The coffee was nutty, rich and the perfect temperature. Although Delaney normally doctored her coffee with cream and sugar, she realized this cup didn't need any help to make it go down smooth. "I'll admit, the fancy gadget makes a great cup of coffee."

Cisco smiled. "I get a little credit, right?"

She wiggled her eyebrows and took another drink. "Maybe. I just want you to know that when you're ready to talk about the meeting, about what you need from me, I can handle it. You can trust me, Cisco."

To her surprise, the color drained from his face. He took off his hat and ran a hand through his hair before meeting her gaze. "Delaney, I want—"

"Are you two going to spend the morning gabbing or are you ready to get to work?"

Delaney turned to see her father standing by the open barn door. "Coming, Daddy," she called, then turned to Cisco. "I'm going to ride out to the southern tip of the ranch to check on the irrigation system. Are you up for it?"

He tipped his head. "Lead on, fearless cowgirl."

Chapter Eight

Cisco stood near the paddock next to the barn a few minutes later, holding the reins of both his and Delaney's horses. She'd gone back to the main house to gather a few snacks in case they were out longer than expected.

He closed his eyes and let the sounds and smells of the ranch wash over him. The fresh scent of hay and animals was quickly becoming something he looked forward to each morning. He'd spent most of his adult life in the big city, rushing from meetings in stuffy conference rooms to site visits in various urban settings. The constant noise and hustle was what he knew, but the appeal of the open plains in Horseback Hollow was quickly growing on him.

"Being on the ranch gives you time to think."

He opened his eyes to find Deke Jones walking toward him.

"It does," Cisco agreed. "It's a welcome change."

"I couldn't imagine being anywhere else," the older man said in his deep, craggy voice. Delaney's father was a true cowboy who represented everything about this town Cowboy Country was trying—unsuccessfully, in Cisco's opinion—to capture about the West.

"Some people don't understand this lifestyle," Deke continued, as if reading Cisco's thoughts. "They think the cowboy way is about flashy belt buckles and blazing guns. There's decades of tradition around these parts. I hate the thought that out-of-towners are going to come in and make a mockery of them."

Cisco swallowed. "I have a great respect for what you do on the ranch, sir."

Deke's gaze flicked to Cisco as if he'd forgotten he was speaking out loud. "You've done good work around here. I saw your dad the other day and told him he should be real proud of you for trying to understand what this town is all about. That's important and shows a good deal of character."

"Thank you, Mr. Jones. It means a lot to me." Cisco felt the warring emotions of pride that a man like Deke Jones would speak so highly of him and guilt over his reason for staying in Horseback Hollow. His professional goals had never been so at odds with his personal desires. He was struggling to figure out how to keep them both moving forward.

"Delaney's had a rough adjustment watching her brothers and sister settle down with their own families. It's left her at loose ends." Deke's blue eyes locked on to Cisco's. "It's made her happy to spend time with you out here on the ranch."

"Your daughter is a special person."

Deke gave a hearty chuckle. "That she is, son." He

tipped his hat, his face turning serious. "As long as you treat her as such, we won't have any problems."

"I don't plan to have any problems," Cisco answered with a nod. His life was becoming more complicated by the second. He was going to have to find a way to explain the whole situation to Delaney before things went any further.

She came bounding around the side of the barn at that moment. "Are you riding out with us, Daddy? It's a beautiful day for it."

"No, darlin'. I need to stay close to the main pasture today." Cisco watched as Deke ruffled Delaney's hair. "Be careful out there. I want you to take a look near the gulches and see if there's any damage from the thunderstorms that rolled in last week."

"You know I can handle it."

Deke shook his head. "It's still smart to be cautious, no matter how good you think you are. Cisco doesn't have as much experience as you."

One side of her mouth curved. "We'll see if he can keep up."

"I mean it, Delaney," Deke said, putting a hand on her shoulder. "Take care." He pointed to Cisco. "Keep an eye on her, son. She can be a handful when she puts her mind to it."

Cisco hid his smile as Delaney's eyes narrowed. "I don't need anyone to keep watch over me. I'm a big girl and plenty capable of taking care of myself."

She stepped away from her father and swung herself into the saddle. Without waiting for Cisco, she gave Flapjack a nudge with her heels as she kissed into the air to spur him on. The big horse took off toward the open field next to the paddock.

"Good luck out there," Deke called as Cisco mounted and turned his horse to follow Delaney.

Cisco waved as he headed away from the barn. "Looks like I'm going to need it," he muttered under his breath.

It took him almost fifteen minutes to catch Delaney. She was never out of his sight but kept a breakneck pace as she wound through the network of trails that led toward the far end of the massive property. He knew it was only because she slowed her horse that he was finally able to come up beside her.

"Your father cares about you," he began, but she held up one hand to stop him.

"I know he cares. I know my family loves me." She adjusted her straw hat lower on her head. "But I'll always be the baby of the family and that's how they still treat me."

"You have more responsibility on the ranch than anyone except your dad."

"Because I'm the only one of the kids left at home."

Cisco shook his head. "There are plenty of people he could find to run things. He trusts you, Delaney."

She brought her horse to a halt. "Thank you," she said, her chest rising and falling with a deep breath.

"It's the truth," he answered.

"I still appreciate you pointing it out. Sometimes my emotions get the best of me."

"I'm happy to remind you of how great you are anytime."

The light in her eyes as she looked at him made his chest tighten. Cisco settled into the saddle as she led him farther along the plains toward the edge of the ranch. He was happy to be with her today, to enjoy her company and forget about everything else that weighed on him for a little bit. Out here with the land and sky both stretching for miles in front of them, Cisco felt as though he and Delaney were the only two people on earth. He knew life wasn't that simple, but it was nice to pretend for a few hours.

The sun shone directly overhead as Delaney hopped off Flapjack and let his reins drop to the ground. The heat today was nothing compared to where it would be in a month or so, but after several hours in the saddle, she'd led them to a copse of pecan trees for a rest.

As Cisco dismounted, she took a blanket and the bundle of food out of her saddle pack, then gave her horse a small pat on the rear. Flapjack moved a few feet to join Cisco's horse grazing in the meadow.

"Drink?" Cisco held out a canteen to her.

The water was cool to her parched throat and she took a long drink, not even caring as a few drops dripped down her chin. She felt Cisco's finger trace the liquid as it soaked into her skin. She choked a little and he patted her back, taking the blanket from her and spreading it on a flat patch of ground.

"You okay?" His voice held a hint of amusement.

She nodded, embarrassed that the heat she suddenly felt had nothing to do with the warm breeze and beating sun.

She knelt on the blanket, busying herself with unwrapping the foil package. "Mama and I made cinnamon bread last night," she told him, clearing her throat. "It's my favorite."

He eased himself down next to her and took a slice. "Very good," he said, resting back on one elbow as he bit into the bread. "Do you often bake?"

She shrugged. "Not as much as I used to, but it's something my mom and I like to do together." She tore off a bite of the bread. "And I like to eat, so it helps to have yummy food around."

"I'd guess that's not a problem at your mother's house?"

Delaney laughed, shaking her head. "She almost always cooks for a crowd. Now that the house is mostly empty, our freezers are full. She also feeds the ranch hands some days. It's a part of who she is."

"A remarkable woman," Cisco supplied, then lay back on the blanket, tipping his hat to shade his eyes.

"She's the best. Everyone in my family is great."

"Tell me more about them."

It was easy to talk about her brothers and sister, their misadventures from childhood and the paths each of them had taken as they grew up. Cisco listened, asking questions occasionally and adding corresponding stories about his family from when they were growing up.

Delaney wrapped the leftover bread as she spoke, trying to keep her hands busy so she wasn't tempted to throw herself on top of the man sprawled out next to her.

She was very tempted. After all, they were alone on a remote part of the property and a coil of awareness simmered between them even now. She half hoped Cisco would reach for her, but he kept his strong arms crossed behind his head as he listened. He seemed totally at ease, which wound up Delaney all the more. Maybe he wasn't as affected by their mutual attraction as she'd thought. Perhaps his interest in the stories from her youth was just so that he could continue to collect more information on the Fortunes, although if that were the case, she still wasn't sure why he didn't go after a wealthier branch of the family.

She wanted to ask him almost as much as she wanted to kiss him again, but neither option seemed appropriate for the moment. Instead she stood and repacked her saddlebag. When she turned, Cisco was standing right behind her, the blanket now folded in his arms.

"These remind me of you," he told her, handing her a small bouquet of wildflowers.

"Thank you." She tucked them in under one of her saddle straps, not wanting him to see the color that rose to her face.

He secured the blanket behind Flapjack's saddle as she moved behind him. "This was a nice break in the day."

"We don't get a lot of them during calving season," she told him, unable to take her eyes off the way his shirt stretched over the muscles in his back as he moved.

He turned at the same time she leaned forward, and she took advantage of the moment to rise onto her toes and brush her mouth across his. He took off his hat, then deepened the kiss but didn't pull her closer. She bunched her hands in his shirt to get nearer to him.

He broke the kiss too soon, blowing out a breath as he ran one hand through his hair.

She wanted more and didn't let him go. She wouldn't let him go.

"Delaney," he whispered. "I don't want to move too fast for you."

"What if you're moving too slow?"

That brought a hint of a smile to his face. "I'll say it again—you are precious to me. But the situation is complicated."

"Why?" she demanded, her fingers holding tighter in the fabric of his shirt. "Because of your big meeting and the fact that you're using me for my connection to the Fortunes?"

His mouth dropped open. "It isn't—"

"Don't bother to deny it, Cisco. Yes, I want to know more about this business deal, but not if it's going to ruin what's between us." She shook her head. "I'll help you with whatever you need, Cisco. Because I want to, not because you're manipulating me into it. I want to get whatever it is over with so we can move on with us."

She expected him to kiss her or put his arms around her or maybe do a little happy dance. Something to let her know that he felt the same way she did.

Instead he walked away. Not far, just a few paces. But Delaney felt the distance as if half of Texas were between them. When he turned back, shadows clouded his eyes.

"I don't deserve you," he said slowly, as if each word was painful to speak. "I know I'm selfish because I want you anyway."

She held out her hands. "I'm right here."

"I want more for you, Delaney, and the business deal is still an issue. I can't share everything with you now." He squeezed his eyes shut, clenching his fists at his sides. "I don't want to take advantage of you."

"Then tell me," she demanded, growing frustrated. "If I'm really important to you, you'll explain what's going on."

Cisco wanted to tell her. He wanted to lay his heart and conscience bare to this woman. To try and be the man she deserved to have in her life.

But something held him back. He'd always been so sure and confident about every aspect of his life, but he wasn't when it came to Delaney. He had no doubt she cared about him. The problem was she cared about the man she believed him to be.

What happened when she found out he was working with Cowboy Country? He was beginning to see that the amusement park's current business philosophy was at direct odds with everything Delaney's family valued. It had seemed so simple when he'd started this arrangement. Have some fun with a very attractive woman, who also happened to be a Fortune, then use his connection to bring the Fortune money to the table for the condos.

Now he saw how convoluted that plan was. Even if Delaney wasn't as opposed to Cowboy Country as some other members of her family, she cherished the peace and serenity of her hometown. His part of the deal, developing the Cowboy Condos, had the potential to change the landscape and culture of this town for years to come.

He had to believe there was a way to make sure the luxury development enhanced the personality of the area instead of taking away from it. At this point, it was up to him to convince Alden Moore, Kent Stephens and the other executives that it was worth the additional time and money it might take to do this deal the right way. He'd already started laying the groundwork with the investment group from Lubbock, but until he had the buy-in from the top brass at Moore Entertainment, Cisco didn't feel secure that his vision would become a reality.

He couldn't share anything with Delaney until then. If the people in town or some of the Fortunes got wind of the plans before he'd addressed their potential concerns, all his plans would be for nothing. Cisco knew he had to keep things under wraps. He'd seen enough real estate deals go south because of rumor or speculation to not want to take a chance on this one.

That still left the matter of how to appease her. "Delaney, will you trust me? I'll tell you everything as soon as I'm able. Until then I want to enjoy our relationship. I don't want to waste a second of my time in Horseback Hollow."

A look he didn't quite understand crossed her face. "You're leaving?"

"Eventually," he said slowly. "Most of my business is based in Miami. You know that."

"Yes, but you're working on a big deal here. Doesn't that mean you'll need to stay close?"

"For now, yes. *Cielo*," he whispered, coming forward to take her hand, "don't look so sad. I'm here now and I don't want to think about anything else but you."

He bent and brushed his lips across her forehead, then down her cheek. He took his time, loving the softness of her skin under his mouth. "Let me take you out to dinner. A real date."

She sighed but at the same time tilted her head back to give him better access. "You don't have to wine and dine me, Cisco. It's not like I'm one of your high-flying girlfriends back home."

He stopped what he was doing, placing his palms on either side of her face as he looked deep into her eyes. "There are no girlfriends back home."

"You know what I—"

"And there are no other women in Horseback Hollow. There's only you, Delaney. Please go out on a date with me?"

She covered his hands with hers. "I'd like that." Her smile was sweet and genuine and made his chest ache with longing. He wanted her to be his, for as long as she'd have him. He was going to make sure this was one deal he didn't lose.

Chapter Nine

"Don't you look lovely." Jeanne Marie glanced up from her book as Delaney walked into the den.

"Thanks, Mom." Delaney pushed her hair off her shoulder. She'd taken the time to curl it tonight, then dressed in a peach-colored sundress with lace trim and a pair of heels she'd bought on a shopping trip to Vicker's Corners but never had an opportunity to wear. Now she wondered if she was going overboard.

"Are people in town going to think I'm an idiot—that I'm just one more of Cisco's groupies?"

Her mother took off her reading glasses. "Do you feel like an idiot when you're with him?"

"I feel like the most beautiful, cherished girl in the world," Delaney said with a wistful sigh.

"Then that's what you should concentrate on, sweetie. That's what people will see."

"But if Rachel is any indication of what the women he normally dates look like, I'm not in the same league."

"Delaney Fortune Jones, you are in a league of your own. Cisco chooses to spend time with *you*. He comes to this ranch and works all day, never leaving your side. He cares for you. Anyone with eyes can see that. Don't sell yourself short."

The doorbell rang at that moment. "How do you always know the right thing to say?" Delaney asked her mother with a smile as she turned toward the front of the house.

"Years of practice," Jeanne Marie murmured.

Unfortunately for Delaney, the heels she'd chosen to wear to impress Cisco weren't as easy to walk in as her normal cowboy boots. She stumbled several times as she made her way to the front door.

He whistled softly as she opened it to greet him. "Hello, beautiful. You look amazing, Delaney." His gaze strayed down her body to her bare legs and she watched as his eyes darkened.

Maybe the heels were a good idea after all.

He held out two bouquets of flowers.

"One would have been enough," she told him.

He laughed. "For you and your mother."

"You're good, Mendoza. She's in the den. Follow me." As Delaney turned, her heel got stuck on the corner of the carpet. She started to slip but Cisco's strong arm came around her waist to hold her steady.

"Whoa there. You okay?"

So much for the heels. "It's these shoes," she answered, slightly breathless at being held so close to him. She wiggled out of his grasp before she made a fool of herself even more. "They take some getting used to."

"Where are your boots?"

"I thought these would be better for our date night."

"Delaney, I asked you out because I want to spend time with you." Cisco tipped up her chin. "You're a cowgirl and I love that about you. You don't have to change for me or try to be something you're not."

"I just wanted to look pretty," she muttered, realizing how ridiculous it sounded now.

"You are beautiful to me because of who you are, not what you wear." Cisco traced his thumb across the seam of her lips. His touch held so much tenderness it made her chest ache. How could she resist this man?

She took a long breath. "If that's the case, then I'm ditching the high heels." She stepped away from him and sank onto one of the lower steps of the staircase. "I was getting a blister anyway."

"Allow me." Cisco dropped to his knees in front of her. Before she could protest, he put down the flowers on the hall table and wrapped one hand around the back of her ankle, lifting her foot. He used his other hand to unstrap the buckle on her heels. His touch was efficient but gentle.

Delaney had to bite down on her lip to keep from moaning out loud when he slipped off the uncomfortable shoe and massaged his knuckles into the arch of her foot.

"Don't do that," he whispered with a harsh chuckle.

"Do what?"

"Abuse the lip that I like so much." His eyes, dark as the perfect slice of chocolate cake, slammed into hers.

She bit down harder, then laughed when he tickled her toes.

He got both shoes off but kept her feet covered with his hands for a few moments. His tanned skin looked bronze against the paler color on her legs. Delaney couldn't stop the mental image that formed of what his hands would look like on other parts of her body.

As if reading her thoughts, he straightened quickly and stepped away from her, picking up a bouquet. "I'll say hello to your mother while you put on your boots."

She ran up to the second floor of the house and grabbed her favorite pair of red cowboy boots from her closet. By the time she came back down the stairs, her mother and Cisco were walking from the den. Her mother's smile was joyful as she looked from the colorful flowers in her hand to Cisco.

"Aren't they beautiful?"

Delaney noticed that Jeanne Marie's cheeks were flushed pink. Leave it to Cisco Mendoza to charm women of every generation. She made a mental note to keep her toddler niece, Piper, away from him. The precocious toddler would be ruined for other men before she was even out of diapers.

"Would you put my bouquet in water along with yours?" Delaney picked up her flowers and handed them to her mother.

"Of course." Jeanne Marie patted Cisco's arm. "You two have fun tonight."

"I'll take good care of her," Cisco promised. "We won't be out late."

Delaney took her purse from a hook on the wall. "I'm twenty-four," she called over her shoulder. "I don't have a curfew anymore."

"I appreciate the thought nonetheless," her mother said.

Cisco followed her out the front door, closing it behind him.

She turned as she got to his car. "I really am a big girl, so you—"

Her words were cut off as he swept her into his arms, lifting her off her feet and pressing his mouth hard to hers. She opened for him as he deepened the kiss. Any doubt Delaney might have had whether Cisco Mendoza found her as irresistible as she did him vanished in that instant. He kissed her as if his life depended on it. She wasn't sure if they stayed like that, exploring each other, for moments or minutes. It was only when the distant sound of the barn door slamming echoed in the quiet of early evening that he slowly released her.

"If I keep you with me too long," Cisco whispered against her hair, "I may never let you go."

Oh. Well. If that didn't make her toes curl with pleasure…

"Where are we going to dinner?" she asked as he reached around her to open the truck's passenger door. "Someplace in Vicker's Corners?"

"The Cantina," he replied as she climbed into the truck. "I thought it would be nice to stay in Horseback Hollow. Is that okay with you?"

"Sure."

As he closed the door, Delaney couldn't help the disappointment that trickled through her. Yes, she loved this town, but she also knew Cisco had taken Rachel Robinson on a date to a fancy restaurant in the nearby town.

He got in behind the steering wheel and turned on the ignition. Before shifting into gear, he leaned over to her. "If you want to go someplace else, that's fine with me, Delaney. I don't care where we are as long as we're together."

She couldn't help but smile at the fact that he'd once again read her mind. In truth, Delaney loved the food at the Cantina and the fun atmosphere of the local restaurant. She'd never found much use for fancy dinners and suddenly understood that Cisco was trying to honor what he thought would make her happy.

"Me, neither," she answered, and gave him another quick kiss. "Besides, I'm starving. Who knows if I could last the whole drive to Vicker's Corners."

When he smiled, she added, "I bet most of the women you take out don't ever eat more than a couple lettuce leaves."

"Most of the women I've taken out don't matter." He started down the gravel driveway and turned toward town. "Only you." He reached across the center console and laced his fingers with hers.

Delaney couldn't remember ever feeling so happy and she knew, even if it all ended after tonight, she'd never forget this time with Cisco.

The Hollows Cantina was busy on a Saturday night, but since Cisco's cousin, Marcus, and his wife, Wendy Fortune Mendoza, owned the restaurant, Cisco and Delaney got a great table near the back that afforded them both privacy and a nice vantage point for people watching. Cisco hadn't been close to his extended family growing up, but he was enjoying getting to know Marcus during his stay in Horseback Hollow.

Although tonight he only had eyes for the woman seated across from him. He took a slow drink of beer and watched Delaney, her eyes shining as she spoke to a high school friend who'd approached the table as their plates were cleared. She knew at least half the people in the restaurant by name and chatted easily, including him in the conversations in a way that made him feel as if he was truly becoming a part of this community. Of course, a number of people already knew his dad and sister, so that helped, as well.

Cisco wondered what these same people would think when they got wind of his work with Cowboy Country. The topic of the theme park and possible related projects had come up several times, although no one seemed to know specifically about the luxury condos he was helping to develop. Locals weren't shy about voicing their concerns and criticism about the way things were being handled by Moore Entertainment. He noticed that Marcus and Wendy didn't offer their thoughts, probably because no matter the concerns they might have, the influx of tourists to the theme park would bring additional business to the Cantina.

Delaney, too, was circumspect in giving her opinion. Cisco was glad she didn't have anything specifically negative to say about the plans. Cowboy Country was due to open in a few weeks, although Cisco knew they were having personnel problems that threatened to derail the whole deal. His resolve to convince Kent and the other executives to pay more attention to the feedback from people in town strengthened.

The more he got to know Horseback Hollow, the more convinced he was that if the community was on board with Cowboy Country, it would help the brand and the experience customers would have when they got to town. He was having trouble getting Kent to see anything beyond the bottom line and had another meeting scheduled with investors in Lubbock to lock them in. Hopefully, that would buy him a little breathing room from the pressure of securing support from the Fortune family.

When he finally presented his case to Delaney, he wanted it to be a strong one. He knew she wouldn't like that he hadn't been up-front with her from the start and he needed to make sure he had a valid explanation for why he'd handled things the way he had.

He gave his head a mental shake and waved as Delaney's friend left the table.

"I'm sorry I've been gabbing with so many people," Delaney said, pulling a face. "That's one of the problems with staying in town. Not much chance of staying incognito in a town this size."

"I like watching you talk to friends and how much you genuinely care about these people. It's clear they feel the same about you. I've never experienced a community like Horseback Hollow. Most of the time in Miami my social interactions relate to my business. It's fun to be out with no hidden agenda."

As soon as the words were out of his mouth, he regretted them. Doubt clouded Delaney's crystal-blue eyes. He hated himself for putting it there.

"No hidden agenda?" she asked drily. "As much as I want to, why do I find that so hard to believe with you, Cisco?" She tapped her fingernails on the side of her water glass as her eyes glinted at him. He saw amusement in them, but also a subtle wariness. "You were lost in thought only a few moments ago. Perhaps contemplating your mysterious business deal and deciding which Fortune to get to know next?"

No other woman had ever been willing to call Cisco out on any of the maneuvering and manipulation that went along with his deal making. Maybe because he'd never let anyone close enough to see who he truly was behind the mask of the smooth-talking real estate developer. That identity had served him well and contributed to his success, but it was useless with Delaney.

"I promise I'll tell you everything about my business in town when the time is right. No matter what, you're the only Fortune who's important to me," he told her, reaching across to take her hand in his. He leaned in and put his lips to her fingertip, warming the skin that was cool from her glass.

Her eyes widened, then darted from side to side as if she worried that someone might notice his obvious display of affection.

"Don't you think it's too late to be concerned about going public?" He held her hand and couldn't care less who saw him do it. Several of the people who'd come over to the table tonight had been men, ranchers or local cowboys, mostly friends of Delaney's brothers'. But Cisco hadn't missed the way they'd looked at her or the glares shot in his direction as her dinner companion.

Delaney might think the guys in this town thought of her as a little sister. Cisco believed it had more to do with their worry over the men in her family standing figurative guard in front of her than lack of interest. Now that he'd ostensibly proven it was possible to take Delaney Fortune Jones on a date and live to tell the tale, he imagined she'd have no shortage of potential suitors nosing around the ranch. He knew her dream was to end up with a true Horseback Hollow man and that his own time in town was limited. It didn't prevent him from wanting to throw a hard right hook at any man who thought about Delaney the way he did.

She stiffened but didn't try to pull back. "Gossip spreads through this town faster than a wildfire on the plains. That much is true. But people know you've been helping out at the ranch. They could think we're coworkers out for a friendly dinner."

He traced his fingers along the inside of her wrist, up her arm to where it bent. He saw her shiver and felt goose bumps rise up where he touched. "I don't want anyone to doubt why I've taken you to dinner, Delaney. I hope we're friends, but that isn't all I want from you. Not by a long shot."

Chapter Ten

Delaney wondered if it was possible for a person to actually melt with desire. She'd never felt anything like the way her body heated at Cisco's touch. What he could do with just his fingers on her arm made her want to crawl across the table and press her whole body to his.

She knew her face must be screaming red and had a feeling more than one table around them was curious about exactly what was going on between her and Cisco. The realization flashed into her mind that when he left Horseback Hollow, she'd be left here with half the town watching her manage a broken heart.

Broken heart? Where had that thought come from? Had she really given her heart to Cisco Mendoza so quickly?

She pulled her hand from his and took a long drink of water, resisting the urge to fan her fingers in front of her face.

"Did I go too far again?" he asked as he watched her.

"No, it's fine." She couldn't begin to admit how far ahead of her brain her heart had galloped. "I want…" She broke off, not sure how to continue without revealing too much. "I'm not sure what I want, but I'm glad we're friends, Cisco."

He nodded. "I hope we'll always be friends."

"Even after you return to Florida?" she couldn't help but ask.

"Have you ever visited Miami?"

She shook her head.

"It's very different from Horseback Hollow, but it's an amazing city. There is so much energy. People have come from all over and made the city a melting pot of cultures. The music and food are amazing."

"I wouldn't fit into your world." Delaney pulled her hair back, then flipped it over one shoulder. "Everyone would think I'm a total country bumpkin."

"People would think you were beautiful and fresh and so alive. Just like I do."

Before Delaney could answer, Marcus Mendoza approached the table again. "How was everything?"

"Perfect," Delaney answered with a smile.

"You've done well for yourself with this restaurant," Cisco told him.

"Thank you," Marcus answered. "How long are you staying in Horseback Hollow before the big city calls you back?"

"Awhile longer."

"You must be working quite a deal."

Delaney saw shock flash in Cisco's eyes before he covered it. "What have you heard?"

Marcus patted him on the shoulder. "Don't worry.

Whatever's going on hasn't leaked yet. I just know from how much Orlando praises your head for business that a guy like you wouldn't be satisfied in a one-horse town like this if there wasn't something going on to sweeten the pot."

Delaney felt herself stiffen. Cisco gave her a reassuring smile. "Horseback Hollow is a great place. I'm in no hurry to leave."

His cousin looked between Cisco and Delaney. "Especially if you find a good enough reason to stay. You'll have to visit our family's place down in Red Rock while you're still in town," Marcus said. "It's a different atmosphere than the Cantina. I think you'd like it."

"We'll try it," Cisco said, reaching out to take Delaney's hand. This time his touch was comforting and she found she liked it just as much.

After they'd said goodbye to Marcus and Wendy, Cisco drove her back to her parents' house. His mood had changed since they'd left the restaurant, as if something about the conversation with Marcus bothered him. He was mostly silent on the way to the ranch, and Delaney couldn't help thinking about Marcus's comment that Horseback Hollow wasn't the right sort of town for Cisco. She wondered for the umpteenth time if a real relationship between them would work, despite her growing feelings for him and the attraction that bubbled just below the surface whenever they were together.

He hopped out of the truck in front of the house and came around to open her door. As he walked her up the steps, Delaney asked, "Do you want to come in for a bit?"

He glanced at his watch. "It's almost eleven. The house is dark, so your parents are probably asleep already. I don't want to make a lot of noise and wake them."

"We don't have to make noise," she blurted, then squeezed shut her eyes. She didn't actually mean the words as a sexual innuendo but they sure came out that way. Why didn't she just throw herself at him? That might be subtler.

She opened her eyes and he smiled, but it looked almost painful. "I had a wonderful time with you tonight, Delaney. As always." He bent and brushed his lips against hers. When she leaned into him, however, he pulled back. His hand cupped her face and he placed a gentle kiss on her forehead. "Sweet dreams, *mi cielo*," he whispered, and took a step back.

Delaney wasn't the most experienced woman on the planet but she could certainly take a hint like that. Cisco wanted to be rid of her. He was trying to be a gentleman about it.

"Good night, then," she said, proud that she kept her voice steady. Without another glance at him, she slipped in the front door, then pressed her back to it. Her breath came in ragged puffs as she dug her fingernails into her palms.

She'd had a great time tonight and refused to end the night in tears. Not over a man.

After a few minutes, Delaney peeked out the curtains at the front window. Cisco still stood in the driveway, hands pressed against the hood of his car. He was cast in shadow from the porch light, a lean silhouette in the darkness. Then he turned and although she couldn't see his eyes under the wide brim of his cowboy hat, the shiver that went through her made her think he was looking straight at her. It was probably just her imagination. The house was dark, so it would be impossible to see her clearly. But he continued to stare and Delaney couldn't move.

Emotion seemed to swirl in the air between them and she wanted so much to run out to him. Just as she took a step, he straightened and climbed into the truck. As she watched, he headed down the driveway and the moment was lost.

Just like her heart, Delaney thought sadly as she made her way up the stairs to her bedroom.

A warm breeze blew without offering much relief from the heat of the morning. Cisco went to readjust his Stetson but realized he'd left it at the rental house when he'd rushed out earlier. Normally he was up with the sun, but after his date with Delaney two nights ago had ended so badly, sleep hadn't come easy the past couple of days. He'd been busy with meetings down in Lubbock, so hadn't been back to the Jones's ranch since then.

He'd called Delaney a couple of times but had gone straight through to her voice mail, leaving him unsure if she was simply busy or avoiding his call. She'd answered his texts with one-word answers, which would have amused Cisco if it weren't so frustrating. In Miami he had no shortage of women vying for his attention but here the one girl he cared about had no problem blowing him off when she thought he deserved it.

Which, in truth, he did. He'd had the most amazing time with her at dinner. It was refreshing to be with Delaney, who seemed to like him best when he wasn't "on." Cisco hadn't realized how much of his life was spent playing a role until he didn't have to anymore. But talking to Marcus had shaken him. His cousin had been right about his motivations for staying in Horseback Hollow, although the longer he was in town, the more his reasons shifted. He was off his game with this real estate deal.

The investors he'd met with yesterday were ready to sign on to the development deal, but they wanted his assurance that everything was on track with the Cowboy Condos before they finalized their involvement. Cisco held back from giving them that and had a meeting scheduled with Kent Stephens and Alden Moore later this afternoon to voice his continuing concerns over how things were being handled. He still believed he could get everything done the right way. To him "right" was more and more defined by not messing up his relationship with Delaney. He'd never before put anything before business and his professional reputation and it scared the hell out of him how important she'd become in his life so quickly.

He walked up to the steps of his sister's house, where he was meeting his brother and father for a late family breakfast. He'd purposely come a few minutes early to get some time with his sister. Gabi greeted him at the door with a hug before punching him softly on the shoulder. "You've got some explaining to do, mister."

Cisco nearly groaned out loud. "You've heard about the date," he muttered.

She took his arm and led him through the cozy ranching house to the kitchen. "I've heard that you were practically peeling off each other's clothes in the middle of the Cantina."

"Who the hell said that?" Cisco planted his feet, temper suddenly flaring. "She's not that kind of a woman and I won't have anyone talking about her like she's playing fast and loose."

"The question is, are *you* playing fast and loose with *her*?"

Cisco glanced over his shoulder to see Matteo coming into the house.

"He'd better not be," Gabi called to their brother. "Delaney is my family now." She took a coffeepot off the counter, then spun to point a finger at Cisco. "You can't play any of your typical games with her."

"What games?" he asked, throwing his hands up. "I like her. We're friends. I took her to dinner."

Gabi made a face. "You know what I mean."

"I know what you mean," Matteo volunteered, elbowing Cisco as he walked by. "My own brother tried to steal my girl."

"I didn't try to steal Rachel," Cisco practically growled. "Hell, we met her on the same day. Once I knew you two were serious, I backed off. Besides, if I hadn't been there to spur you on, who knows how long it would have taken you to make a move."

"So I should thank you?" Matteo asked drily.

"I didn't say that." Cisco paced to the edge of the kitchen and back. "Am I really that bad that even my brother and sister doubt my intentions?"

Matteo flashed a grin. "Is that a rhetorical question?"

"We love you," Gabriella said quickly. "And we want to trust you. But Delaney's special, Cisco. She's got a lot of spirit, but not as much experience with men."

"I'm not going to hurt her." He said the words slowly, like a promise, sending up a silent prayer that he could keep it.

"Who got hurt?" Orlando ambled into the kitchen, taking the steaming mug Gabi offered. "I've seen just about every doctor within a fifty-mile radius, so if they need recommendations…"

"Not that kind of hurt, Dad," Matteo told him. "We're

talking about Don Juan Mendoza over there and Delaney Fortune Jones."

Orlando nodded at Cisco. "Heard you two had a pretty steamy dinner at the Hollows Cantina the other night."

"See?" Gabi handed Cisco a cup of coffee. "There are no secrets in this town."

"If you say so."

"At least not for long," she added as she studied him.

He felt a muscle twitch in his jaw and tried to rein in his frustration. He wasn't used to being called on the carpet. Cisco had pretty much lived life by his own terms since he could remember. His family didn't meddle in his life, and he left them alone. Living in a small community sure had rubbed off on them fast.

"I like Delaney," he said, then took a drink of coffee to wet his suddenly dry throat before setting it on the counter. "A lot. I respect her, too. Her whole family."

Gabi gave him a gentle push toward the kitchen table. "I actually believe you."

He slipped into a chair, massaging his temples as he did. Orlando sat next to him and Matteo across the table. Gabi put a plate of bacon in the center of the table along with an egg casserole that smelled delicious. His sister was as good of a cook as their mother had been. Sitting with his family like this made Cisco miss his mom even more. She'd always been the center of their family. He knew it would have made her happy to have them together for a meal.

"Is Jude joining us?"

Gabi shook her head, then took a seat next to Matteo. "He left early this morning for one of the far pastures with his dad. I don't expect to see him until dinnertime." She picked up the plate of bacon. "Dig in, you three. It's such a treat to have all of us together. I wish Alejandro and Joaquin could be here, too."

"You never know," Orlando said as he scooped a big helping of eggs onto his plate. "If we can convince them to visit, Horseback Hollow is hard to resist once you're here."

"Even Cisco is staying busy," Matteo added. "How's work on the ranch?"

"I'm learning a lot." Cisco took a bite of the casserole. "I have a ton of respect for Deke Jones and what he's built, how hard he and his crew work. Gabi, you understand with Jude being a rancher."

She and their father both nodded. "Deke and Jeanne Marie are good people," Orlando said after taking a drink of coffee. "All of the Fortunes, actually."

Cisco thought about asking his father if he was referring to one of the British Fortunes in particular but held off. He didn't appreciate the third degree about Delaney, so he didn't want to do the same to Orlando.

"Does that mean you're thinking of trading in your real estate license for a branding iron?" Matteo asked, mimicking the action of branding cattle in the air in front of him.

"Not quite," Cisco answered.

"I knew it." Matteo pointed to him with a bacon strip. "You're working a deal."

"What makes you think—?"

"You get a certain look on your face. Always have since you were a kid."

Gabi gave a soft laugh. "Remember the window-cleaning business you started when Dad was stationed out in California? You made the sales and had the rest of us working for you all summer."

Cisco couldn't help but smile at the memory. "Every great entrepreneur needs minions underneath him. You were perfect for that role."

"But it's bigger now. I can tell." Matteo leaned back in his chair. "What's going on around Horseback Hollow that could possibly hold your interest?"

"Besides Delaney Fortune Jones?" Orlando added with a wink. "I'd think a good woman was quite enough."

"Not for Cisco," Matteo said. "He's the king of the million-dollar deal. But I can't figure out what could hold his attention…" He broke off as his eyes widened. "Unless…"

"Isn't it enough that I'm here?" Cisco asked impatiently.

"Of course it is," Gabi said, taking on their mother's role of peacemaker.

"You're involved with Cowboy Country." Matteo shook his head, pointing his fork at Cisco.

Both Orlando and Gabriella turned to look at Matteo. "What did you say?" their father asked.

"He's got a deal cooking with Cowboy Country. That has to be it. There's nothing else here to keep his interest for so long."

"His family is enough," Orlando stated.

"And Delaney," Gabi added. "It's clear he's fallen for her."

"I'm sitting right here," Cisco told them, not bothering to hide his irritation. "You don't have to talk about me like I'm not in the room."

"Exactly." Orlando placed his coffee on the table and pointed to Cisco. "Tell your brother he's mistaken, that you aren't involved with those outsiders at Moore Entertainment."

"Dad, you say that like you were born and raised in Horseback Hollow. Our family doesn't have roots in this town any more than the people at Cowboy Country."

"Oh, no," Gabi muttered, placing her head in her hands.

"We're different," Orlando argued. "The Mendozas may not have long ties to Horseback Hollow, but we understand the values this town stands for and we—at least some of us—want to protect the community from a corporation that could destroy the very things that make this place special."

"That's a little overly dramatic." Cisco stood, walking to the edge of the counter. "There are some good things that will come from the theme park opening—more jobs, money pumped into the local economy. Maybe folks could start looking at the positive outcomes."

"Money isn't the only factor," his father argued from the table.

"What does Delaney think of your involvement?" Gabi asked quietly.

"And what exactly *is* your involvement?" Matteo added more forcefully. "You've never been so hush-hush about your business ventures before. Why the covert ops this time around?"

"Maybe to avoid the third degree from everyone," Cisco suggested. "I can't give details on exactly what's happening until plans are finalized."

"Then you *are* working for Moore Entertainment?" The disappointment in his father's tone was clear.

"It was a great opportunity and allowed me to stay in Horseback Hollow to spend more time with all of you." Cisco ran his hands through his hair, shaking his head. "I thought that would be a good thing."

"Of course we're glad you're in town." Orlando stood and wrapped an arm around Cisco's shoulder.

"I didn't understand how much people around here were against the theme park until after I started," Cisco added. "I still believe Cowboy Country and the other projects related to it will be a benefit in the long run."

"Do me a favor," Gabi said, "and don't mention that to Jude. He and his brothers can go on for ages about all the reasons Cowboy Country is signaling the apocalypse for Horseback Hollow." She placed her fork on the table and narrowed her eyes. "But you knew that already. You also knew, thanks to me, that not all of the Fortunes were opposed to the theme park."

Cisco held up a hand. "It isn't what you think, Gabriella."

She raised a brow at him and he was again reminded of his mother. Luz Mendoza used to communicate volumes without saying a word.

"Okay, it started out how you think, but I care about Delaney." He looked at his father and brother. "A lot. I would never do anything to hurt her."

"You'd better not or Jude and her other brothers will string you up. Does she know the details of your association with Cowboy Country?"

"Not yet," Cisco admitted. "But I'm sure I can make her understand."

Matteo nabbed the last strip of bacon and began clearing plates off the table. "If anyone can sweet-talk his way out of girl trouble, it's you, Cisco." He gave Cisco a nudge as he walked to the sink. "Rachel thinks of Delaney as a friend, so the Fortune Jones brothers might have to get in line if she's upset by you."

"I think we've made our point," Orlando said, giving Cisco's shoulder another squeeze. "If Cisco tells us his intentions are in the right place, we can trust him. It makes me happy to think you've found a woman to truly care about, son."

"Thanks, Dad." Orlando's thick hair was heavily streaked with silver now, but his father was still the strongest, best man Cisco had ever met. He didn't want to disappoint Orlando. Besides, his feelings for Delaney were definitely real.

He pitched in with everyone to clean up the rest of the dishes. It was comforting and familiar to be with his family in this way and, thankfully, the conversation turned to Gabi and Matteo and what was going on in their lives. Both of his siblings were clearly satisfied with the lives they were creating in Horseback Hollow.

Cisco was happy for them and wondered again if he'd made a mistake in putting so much focus on his career. He hadn't realized how out of balance his life had become until Delaney had become a priority to him. He was used to being focused only on getting ahead, but now that didn't feel nearly as important as making her happy.

Chapter Eleven

"What's wrong?"

The Horseback Hollow Grill was filled with the lunch-time crowd. Delaney had gotten lost in thought watching people at the other tables and barely registered her brother Galen's question. While she knew many of the customers at the popular restaurant, for once in her life there were more people at the Grill who were strangers to her. She attributed that to the influx of new folks working for Cowboy Country. Curiosity always got the best of her in these kinds of situations, but today her mind was occupied with more personal musings. She blinked several times to clear her head, then met Galen's concerned gaze.

"Are you sick?" Galen reached out one long arm to press his knuckles to her forehead. "You don't have a fever. Want me to call Mom and drive you back to the ranch?"

"I'm not sick and nothing's wrong." She took a sip of her soda. "Why do you ask?"

As he lowered his hand, he grabbed several fries from her plate. "Because you've barely touched your grilled cheese and maybe eaten two fries the entire time we've been here."

She shrugged. "I'm not that hungry."

"Exactly my point." He popped a fry in his mouth. "You've got a bigger appetite than Jude and Toby combined most of the time. Something's wrong. I'm guessing you want to talk about it, which is why I was summoned for this lunch."

"I *invited* you," she answered, wrinkling her nose. "That's different than a summons." She picked up half of her sandwich with every intention of taking a bite to prove Galen wrong. The problem was that food held no appeal, so she dropped her favorite sandwich back to the plate. That wasn't a good sign. Galen was right, so she figured she might as well cut to the chase.

"How can you tell if a guy is into you?"

Galen coughed several times. "Geez, Delaney, give me a little warning next time. I can't believe you asked me that question."

"Who else am I supposed to ask?" She threw up her hands. "I need the opinion of a man, someone who knows what he's talking about."

Galen took a long drink of his soda. "I definitely know what I'm talking about."

She gave him an indulgent smile. "Plus you're single. I can't talk to any of the other brothers. Falling in love has changed them."

"Made them soft," Galen agreed with a laugh.

"Don't let them hear you say that." Delaney took a fry,

dipped it in ketchup and took a bite. "But really, Galen, what makes a guy sure that he wants a girl?"

Her brother went suddenly serious. "Maybe you should have this talk with Mom, Delaney. If you don't understand—"

"Stop." Delaney held her hands over her ears for a moment. "I'm not talking about wanting to bed a woman, you dumb cowboy. I mean how can I tell if a man is interested in more than that? When he gets serious about long term. Wedding, not bedding. Does that make sense?"

"I understand what you're asking," Galen answered, looking relieved. "I'm just not sure I have an answer. Why do you think I'm still single? Guys like to keep things simple, but when love gets involved, life gets complicated."

"Tell me about it." Delaney shook her head.

"Is this about Cisco Mendoza?"

Delaney felt color rush to her cheeks. "What do you know about Cisco?"

"Dad mentioned he was working at the ranch."

"Dad talked to you about Cisco?" Delaney was shocked. Deke Jones was notoriously a man of few words.

"Not like you're thinking. It's Dad, after all." Galen picked up the uneaten half of her sandwich. "But he likes Cisco and more important, he respects him. He did say he'd been mostly helping you, so it doesn't take a genius to figure out what's going on." He took a bite. "Any man who spent time with you couldn't help but fall for you, Delaney."

"You're only saying that because you're my brother."

"I'm saying that because you're an amazing girl. What I'll say as your brother is that if Cisco hurts you, I'll string him up with my bare hands. He'll wish he never stepped foot west of the Mississippi."

"I can take care of myself, Galen." Still, Delaney felt a rush of affection for her big, burly brother. "Do you think he likes me? For real?"

"I don't know Cisco personally, but of course I think he likes you. That doesn't necessarily mean he's going to know what to do about it."

"So I should take matters into my own hands?"

Galen choked again just as the waitress came to the table to clear their plates. Delaney watched as the young woman smiled at Galen, who was now gulping down water. The waitress was clearly interested in her older brother, who was just as clearly clueless.

When the woman walked away, Galen leaned forward across the table. "I am *not* telling you to take matters into your own hands."

"I think you're right. If Cisco has feelings for me but isn't going to act on them, it's up to me to show him the way. He needs to understand how I feel and then maybe it will be easier for us to move forward."

"How *do* you feel, Delaney?"

For all of her worry over this, when it came down to it, Delaney was clear about her feelings. She took a deep breath and whispered, "I love him."

Galen rolled his eyes. "So much for the last two single Fortune Jones siblings."

"I didn't plan it."

"Then don't rush into anything. Take it slow. You're young and Cisco is the first guy you've had serious feelings for. How do you know it isn't just a spring fling? You don't want to take a chance and end up hurt. No one wants to see you hurt, Delaney."

Galen's words made a sliver of doubt pass through her. "Of course I don't want to be hurt," she agreed, tying the paper wrapper from her straw into a knot. "If I don't risk it, I may never know if Cisco and I could have something great. He's not going to be in Horseback Hollow forever."

"That's part of my point."

"Maybe," she continued as if her brother hadn't spoken, "I haven't given him enough incentive to stay." An idea popped into her head at that moment. She suddenly knew what her next step had to be.

"Whatever you're planning," Galen said, giving her his best big brother stare, "don't do it."

"What makes you think—?"

"It's that gleam in your eye. It means trouble."

"That's not true," Delaney said as she slid out of the booth.

Galen followed her toward the front of the restaurant. They both waved to friends as they went.

"Whatever happened to your plan to fall in love with a local boy? Cisco might be willing to help on the ranch while he's visiting, but he's not a cowboy at heart. Are you going to change enough to accommodate his life?"

"I love him," Delaney repeated as she adjusted her sunglasses on her nose, happy for the small barrier from Galen's knowing gaze. "Right now that's what matters the most."

"There are at least three single cowboys sitting in the Grill right now. It would be easier for you to stick with what you know."

"That's what I always thought, too." They walked to the end of the block, where Delaney had parked one of the ranch's trucks. She had supplies to pick up in town after she left Galen. "Now I understand there are more important things than the easy way out. If I don't take a risk, I'll always wonder if I could have done more."

"Like I said before, love is way too complicated. I'm here if you need anything, but I'll stick to simpler pleasures, thank you very much."

Delaney stood on her tiptoes to give Galen a quick hug. "Be careful about tempting fate, big brother."

The next morning Delaney shoved Stacey's tube of lip gloss into her jeans pocket before heading down the stairs. She knew it was silly. Ranch life was dusty and dirty most of the time, and there was no need to look her best just to ride under the hot sun all day.

Since her talk with Galen, she'd been able to keep her mind on little else besides Cisco. The whole truth was he'd consumed her thoughts since that first night at her parents' barbecue. Now she could hardly wait to tell him how she felt.

She knew she hadn't imagined his feelings for her, especially the attraction that smoldered between them. But Delaney believed it was more than just physical desire. She and Cisco had an undeniable connection. She loved her life on the ranch, but he made her think about a future outside the one she'd planned for herself. It was terrifying and exhilarating at the same time. There was a good chance she was opening herself up for heartache, but it was worth the risk.

Cisco had gone out of his way to make himself a part of her life. She owed him the same consideration. If he knew she loved him enough to change, maybe that would open the door for him to truly admit his feelings for her.

She grabbed an apple from the kitchen counter and hurried out the door. Her mother would definitely notice that she'd put on makeup and curled her hair this morning. Delaney wasn't ready to deal with Jeanne Marie's good-natured scrutiny. Her phone trilled as she got to the barn. She fished it out of her back pocket and read a text from Cisco that said he was preparing for a meeting and would try to get to the ranch by lunch or he'd call her later tonight.

Delaney stomped her boot into the dirt in front of the barn door. She'd fixed herself up for nothing. Even if Cisco showed up later today, her makeup would be melted off within an hour. It was stupid that she'd made the effort in the first place. If Cisco had real feelings for her, a little bit of mascara and curl to her hair wasn't going to make a difference. He was used to being with women who were more glamorous taking out the trash than Delaney was when she tried her hardest. A lump knotted her stomach at the thought. Was she kidding herself that her simple life could ever make him happy?

Her father and one of the ranch hands were deep in conversation near the horse stalls as she entered. The young cowboy did a double take as his mouth dropped open.

Deke glanced at her, his eyebrows raised.

"Not a word, Daddy." She took a hair band off her wrist and quickly braided her hair down the back. "Please."

Her father gently elbowed the ranch hand next to him. "Eyes back in your head, boy. That's my baby you're drooling over."

The young man snapped shut his mouth. "Yes, sir. Sorry, Delaney," he added, his gaze trained on the ground. "I'll round up the other guys."

As he walked away, emotion clogged Delaney's throat. At least someone appreciated her efforts.

"Cisco coming today?" her dad asked.

"Maybe later. He's getting ready for an important meeting." She didn't bother to hide the bitterness in her tone.

"Too bad," Deke murmured. "We've got a situation out at the far end of the property. One of the calves born last week is missing. I want everyone to split up to canvass as big of an area as we can. The longer that baby is on his own—"

"I'll head out to the north pasture. There are so many hills and valleys out there where a calf could get lost."

"Let me get one of the guys to go with you."

"I'll be fine on my own."

"Delaney—"

"Come on, Daddy. If Jude or Toby rode out alone, you wouldn't have a problem with it. I can cover just as much ground by myself, so it's a waste to bring someone with me."

He looked as if he wanted to argue, so she added, "Please, Dad. I need to clear my head."

Deke sighed heavily. "It's hard for me to believe, but you're not a little girl anymore."

"I haven't been for a long time."

When her father nodded, Delaney stepped forward to place a quick kiss on his tanned cheek. It was huge for her dad to trust her this way. Deke shooed her away but one side of his mouth quirked. Deke Jones could appear remote at times, but he loved his children, and as the baby of the family, Delaney had a closer relationship with him than some of her siblings.

"Take care," he called as she headed quickly to Flapjack's stall.

"I learned from the best." She didn't waste time saddling up her horse and heading out.

Even though she rode Flapjack hard for miles, it took Delaney a fair bit of time to reach the edge of the property. There were places where the typically flat terrain turned hilly, with dry creek beds carved out of the land. She slowed her horse to a walk, pausing every few minutes to scan the horizon and listen for any sounds. The calf should still have been following its mother, and Delaney knew if they didn't find it soon, the animal would be an easy target for a predator in the area.

As she rode, she tried to keep her mind focused totally on the lost baby and not on her heart, which she feared might also be forever lost. Although it didn't make sense, somehow the idea of finding the calf was tied inexorably in Delaney's mind to her own fate. As if by keeping the animal safe, she could somehow ensure her own future happiness.

She'd spent a good portion of her childhood in these sorts of musings, but as she began working the land with her siblings, her father had made it clear there was no room for flights of fancy on the ranch. Shaking her head to bring herself back to her senses, Delaney heard a faint noise over the next rise. As she got closer, Flapjack picking his way carefully over rivets and through underbrush, the sound became a distinct bleating. The calf stood to one side of a distant clump of trees, standing still except for bobbing its neck forward with the despairing cry.

Not wanting to spook the animal, Delaney dismounted about ten feet away and began moving slowly forward. She held a rope in one hand and spoke in her most soothing tone, promising the calf a reunion with his mother and all the milk he could drink. As she got closer, the calf's cries got louder and he went to move away, only to stumble. She held her breath as he righted himself. Then she glanced back at Flapjack. She'd brought along a satellite walkie-talkie to radio back to her father but left it in her saddlebag in her excitement to reach the lost calf. She decided she'd secure the calf, then take care of the communication.

The baby tensed as she got closer but seemed to relax when he realized she didn't mean him any harm. Caressing the downy fur behind his ear, she looped the rope over his head and knelt beside him. There seemed to be no real injuries as she ran her hands along his legs, flank and belly. Delaney breathed a sigh of relief and took off her hat, then rested her forehead on the animal's fur. His heart rate raced, then calmed as her breathing steadied.

Another sound captured her attention. She glanced over her shoulder and her breath caught again. Tucked under one of the nearby cypress trees was a nest made from sticks and branches. Peeking out were four tiny snouts. A nest of wild hogs. Maybe the calf had wandered close to the other little ones for companionship, but Delaney had to get them both away before the mama returned. Feral hogs were a problem all across Texas. They did their best on the ranch to keep the property clear of the destructive animals, but it was difficult to monitor every inch of the land, especially this far out from the main pastures.

She straightened and tugged on the rope just as Flapjack gave a distressed whinny. She turned to see an enormous wild boar charge out of the underbrush toward her horse. Flapjack reared up but the mother hog kept running at him. Delaney screamed, drawing the sow's attention, then watched as her horse galloped away.

There was no time to wrap her mind around that as the babies behind her started squealing, obviously sensing that their mother and a meal were nearby.

She tried to shush them as the sow paused to check her out. "Be quiet. We don't want mama pig to think I'm causing problems," she commanded in a gentle tone.

Her baby-whisperer voice didn't work on the piglets as it did on her niece, and their squealing continued. The huge sow stomped her front foot on the ground several times and squealed at Delaney. The last place she wanted to be right now was between that mother and her babies. She pulled on the rope again, but the calf only bleated louder, as if crying for his own mama.

Left with no other option, she turned and hefted the animal into her arms, staggering a bit as she moved. Delaney was strong, but the calf probably weighed close to seventy pounds. Fear and adrenaline kept her going and she sidestepped away from the piglets, never taking her eyes off the sow. When she'd made it about five feet away, she turned and did her best to run over the closest rise, wanting to get herself and the calf out of the hog's line of sight. Although unable to see the ground in front of her with her arms full of animal, it was still a shock when she stepped into a hole and her ankle twisted.

Dropping to one knee, then onto her backside, Delaney managed to keep a tight hold on the baby, which bleated in protest. Her gaze darted over her shoulder but, thankfully, the mama hog hadn't followed her. Delaney hugged the calf against her and her heart rate eventually calmed. She released the baby but kept the rope clenched between her fingers.

As her breathing slowed, pain replaced fear and she took stock of her various injuries. She gently turned her ankle and although it hurt, she didn't think it was broken. Her jeans were ripped at the knee, dirt and pebbles embedded in her skin where she'd gone down. The underside of her arm was also scraped, plus her hip ached from where she'd landed on a rock. All told, they were surface injuries and she knew she was lucky they weren't worse, especially since she had a very long walk back to the main house.

She glanced at the calf, which continued to watch her out of big brown eyes. Her best hope was that Flapjack would return to the barn. The chances of the calf having the strength to make it back were slim, and Delaney was afraid to leave the pitiful creature out here on its own.

Careful to keep far away from the feral hogs, Delaney started in the direction of home. Clouds gathered above her in the sky, signaling an impending spring rain. She was grateful for the reprieve from the hot sun but didn't relish the idea of being caught out in a storm on the open land.

She walked for an hour, then found shade under a tree to rest. The calf had stopped making noise a mile or so back and Delaney wished she had some way to hydrate him. Her own throat was dry and caked with dust and her ankle was beginning to throb in her boot. All she could hope was that her father and the ranch hands would find them sooner rather than later.

A brief rest might help revive her energy, so she moved rocks and sticks away from where she sat and lay back on the hard ground. As her eyes drifted shut, she wondered briefly if Cisco had arrived at the ranch, and how he'd react to her being gone. Since he'd pretty much blown her off this morning, would he even care?

Chapter Twelve

Thunder rumbled overhead in an ominously black sky. Raindrops pelted the truck's front window, hard but intermittent for now. Cisco knew that wouldn't last. Any minute he expected the heavens to open up and drench the land in one of the intense spring thunderstorms this part of the country was known for. He had to find Delaney before that happened.

He'd spent the morning retooling the presentation he planned to give to Alden Moore and Kent Stephens this afternoon. Based on the concerns about Cowboy Country that reverberated throughout Horseback Hollow, Cisco was making a case to upgrade the theme and design of the development to make the condos less hokey cowboy and pay more homage to authentic Western history. There was certainly enough of that around town and in the region to draw on for inspiration.

He'd even contacted the firm tasked with drawing plans for the condos to see how they felt about incorporating the changes. The architect in charge had been all for it, and Cisco believed this was his chance to turn his real estate plans into something that even the most cynical Fortune could appreciate. At the very least he thought it would make Delaney happy.

Guilt ate at him now because he hadn't been with her this morning. Deke had told him she'd insisted on riding out by herself, and the craggy rancher's unspoken censure had told Cisco that the fault for that lay squarely on his shoulders.

The walkie-talkie on the seat next to him crackled as one of the ranch hands checked in with the search party. No one had spotted Delaney yet. Her horse had just returned to the barn with no rider when Cisco'd arrived. Deke had spared no time in organizing all available men to go after her. Some rode out on horseback. A couple took one of the ranch's ATVs. Cisco had grabbed a walkie-talkie from Deke and taken off in his truck. He could cover more ground driving, although there were places on the ranch he couldn't reach. He only hoped Delaney had been able to make it to one of the open areas where she'd be easier to spot. She was strong and knew her way around the land, two things that would work to her advantage—assuming she wasn't hurt or in real trouble.

The fear that shot through him at that thought had him punching the gas pedal. He leaned forward over the steering wheel to scan the area. As the rain turned to a fine drizzle, a flicker of color caught his eye far in the distance. He slowed the truck, then grabbed the binoculars Deke had handed him on his way out of the barn and trained his view to the spot ahead. After a few seconds of focusing, Delaney came into view, slowly walking in his direction with the lost calf tied to a rope behind her.

Cisco traded the binoculars for the walkie-talkie and radioed in to Deke that he'd found her and would meet everyone back at the barn. Because of the uneven terrain, his pace in the truck was slow. Eventually he got close enough that she spotted him, waving her hands above her head while he beeped the horn in response.

When he came to a ravine too deep for the truck to cross, he went the rest of the way on foot, moving as fast as he could through the underbrush that covered this part of the property.

She gave him a small, tired smile as he got close. "Fancy meeting you—" she started to say, but Cisco grabbed her up into a tight hug, and she buried her face in his neck, her hands fisting in his shirt.

"Delaney," he whispered, "are you okay? What happened? I can't believe I wasn't here."

"If you put me down, I'll explain," she said, her breath soft on his throat. "But…um…Cisco, I kind of can't breathe with you holding on so tight."

He forced himself to release her, placing her gently back down on the ground. "When I got to the ranch, your horse had just returned to the barn without you."

"Good boy," she said. "That's what I hoped he'd do."

"I don't understand."

"I found the calf and had gone over to secure him but ended up between a feral hog mama and her babies. She spooked Flapjack, and he took off. Unfortunately, my walkie-talkie was still in the saddlebag."

Cisco cupped his hands over her cheeks, smoothing a

stray hair away from her jaw. "I should have been with you."

She shrugged her shoulders. "You had a meeting to prepare for."

"It's not as important as you. Nothing is as important as you." The realization hit him like a leaded weight. His career was all he'd cared about for most of his adult life, but work no longer meant a thing if it compromised Delaney in the process.

"You're here now," she offered, always willing to see the best in him even if he didn't deserve it. "You came to find me."

His heart squeezed when a single tear tracked down her face. She was so beautiful to him, so precious. He'd stayed in Horseback Hollow to make a deal but had discovered something more important in the process.

The calf standing behind her let out a plaintive bleat, reminding Cisco that they had the current reality to deal with before he could really talk to her. Despite her smile, Delaney was clearly exhausted. He needed to get her and the calf back to the ranch.

He couldn't resist lifting her fingers to his lips. Her delicate hands fascinated him, and he longed to give her body the same sweet attention all over. Then he noticed the red scrape down the side of her forearm.

"You're hurt." He took a step away and saw that her jeans were ripped at the knee. A raw, angry cut slashed across her skin.

"Just a few scratches." She held up her arm for inspection. "I twisted my ankle a bit, too. I hope we won't have to cut off my boot. They're my favorite pair."

Anger flared bright inside him, anger at himself that he hadn't been with her on this ride. She'd been hurt and he knew much of the blame lay with him. Certainly Deke Jones would think that.

"I'm going to take care of you, Delaney." He took the rope from her hand and scooped her up, one arm behind her back and the other at her knees.

She gave a startled squeak. "I appreciate the gesture," she said quickly as he began to move. "But I can handle it and I'm not sure the calf has enough strength left to walk. You should put me down and try him if you're really looking to be a hero."

"First things first." Cisco dropped the rope and continued toward the truck. He could feel Delaney watching him but kept his gaze trained on the ground in front of them. No need for both of them to go down. He also didn't quite trust himself to look at her or speak. Too much emotion jumbled around inside of him.

He maneuvered the passenger-side door open and with as much care as possible deposited Delaney on the seat. He turned to go back for the calf, but she reached out and smoothed her fingers along his face.

They trailed to the back of his neck as she pulled him forward and placed a soft kiss on his mouth. "You're *my* hero," she whispered.

The emotion in her eyes made anything he had to give up professionally to be with this woman worth the sacrifice.

At that moment a huge crack of thunder reverberated through the sky and lightning flashed on the horizon. Rain began to pound the earth in earnest, so Cisco shut the door to the truck and ran as fast as he could back to the calf, hefting the animal into his arms as he made his way to the truck again. Deke had thrown an old barn blanket in the back bed. The poor baby was so fatigued that it practically collapsed onto the heavy flannel. Cisco arranged the calf as best he could before the rain turned into a downpour, then rushed to climb behind the wheel.

Delaney was speaking to her father on the walkie-talkie as he started the engine.

"Yes, Daddy, I'm fine," she told Deke. "We should be home in about twenty minutes. Tell Mama I love her."

"He was really worried," Cisco said as she turned off the walkie-talkie and set it on the console between them. He wiped his sleeve across his drenched face, then took her hand in his. "We all were."

"I can take care of myself," Delaney said.

"I know you can," he answered. "Doesn't stop the worry."

After a moment she scooted close enough to lay her head on his shoulder. "I could get used to you worrying about me, Mr. Mendoza."

Her simple pronouncement melted his heart. "I sure hope so."

Although the ride back to the ranch was bumpy, Delaney almost fell asleep on Cisco's shoulder. It felt so right to lean on him for support. As the baby of her family, Delaney had spent a lot of time in life trying to prove she could hold her own, so it was a nice change to let someone else be strong.

She'd always thought that relying on a man would make her feel weak, the way she did sometimes with her brothers. But it seemed natural to let Cisco take care of her. The fact that he'd been so worried and then grateful when he found her gave her confidence that he returned her feelings, even if neither of them had spoken the words out loud.

She wanted to change that, but as they pulled closer to the house, she realized it would have to wait. The rain had stopped, so her parents were waiting in the driveway. As soon as the car stopped, Jeanne Marie hurried toward her door. Delaney climbed out, stiff from her fall and the subsequent hike across the pastures now that the adrenaline had worn off. Her body ached from head to toe and while she tried not to put much weight on the ankle she'd twisted, she was grateful for her mother's warm embrace.

"You gave us such a fright," Jeanne Marie whispered. "Thank heavens you're safe."

"I've sent some of the guys out there to trap that feral hog and her babies." Her father stood a few steps behind her mother. His face was a solid mask of strength, but Delaney could see emotion burning in his eyes. "I thought we had them under control on the property but it's a constant battle."

"It's okay, Daddy." She stepped away from her mother toward the back of the truck. "The calf's going to need a lot of help. From what I can tell, he's severely dehydrated."

Deke looked relieved to have someplace productive to put his attention. "I'm proud of you, Delaney, for how you handled today."

The compliment from her normally tight-lipped father made Delaney's throat squeeze with emotion. "You were right, though. I shouldn't have gone all the way out there alone."

"It all turned out well." Her father patted her arm as he slid by her, a huge display of affection from Deke Jones. "That's what counts."

"Let's get you in the house," Jeanne Marie said, keeping her arm around Delaney's shoulders.

She glanced over her shoulder to where Cisco stood near the side of the truck. "I'll help your dad settle the calf, then come and check on you."

Delaney nodded and let her mother lead her toward the ranch house. Her braid stuck to the back of her neck thanks to the post-rain humidity clinging to the air. She struggled on the front steps a bit and her mother leaned in closer.

"I can do it, Mama. The stairs are just a bit tricky. My ankle needs a rest."

"Every part of you needs a rest and I'm going to make sure you get it." Jeanne Marie opened the door and helped Delaney through the front of the house to the couch in the cozy den. "We'll start here and then you can head upstairs for a shower when you're feeling up to it." She stepped back, her gaze focusing on Delaney's injuries. "Do I need to call the doctor?"

"Definitely not," Delaney told her, leaning her head back on a sofa cushion. "I got a little banged up when I fell." After a moment she sat up again. "But I could use some help with my boots."

"I can do that." Cisco appeared behind her mother. "Deke sent me in here to check on Delaney."

Jeanne Marie turned and gave him a quick hug. "Thank you so much for finding our girl. If you'll stay with her awhile longer, I'm going to get the first-aid kit and put on a pot of tea."

"Of course," he answered. "I'll take good care of her."

"I know you will." Jeanne Marie patted Cisco's arm, then came forward to drop a gentle kiss on the top of Delaney's head. "I'll be back in a few minutes. Call if you need anything."

As her mother slipped out of the room, Cisco walked

forward a few steps. "It kills me to see you like this. If you want to go upstairs, I can carry you so you don't have to take the steps with your ankle."

"It's fine," she whispered. The thought of Cisco carrying her up to her bedroom, even for the most innocent reasons, left her breathless.

His eyes darkened even more and he shook his head, as if reminding himself to stay focused. "We need to deal with the boots."

She bit down on her lip and nodded. "I can manage the first one."

She started to lean forward but he dropped to his knees in front of her. "Lean back." He gave her shoulder a gentle push. "You've done enough today." This was the second time he'd knelt in front of her and again it made Delaney feel a bit like a princess. She never would have pegged herself for the fairy-tale type, but she was loving Cisco's attention.

He pulled off the first boot with ease, but as he tugged at the second, Delaney gave a muffled cry as white-hot pain radiated up her leg. Her hand flew to cover her mouth. "It's okay," she said through her fingers. "I'll be fine."

"I don't want to hurt you." Cisco's mouth was set in a grim line. He gently touched her ankle through the leather, then set her foot on the couch and straightened. "I'll be right back."

As he disappeared out of the room, Delaney's eyes closed. She wiped the sweat from her brow with one sleeve. She didn't want to be a wimp, but the pressure on her ankle when he moved the boot was almost too much to stand.

Cisco walked back in a few minutes later, carrying

a tray that held a tall glass of water, several washcloths and a bag of ice, plus a plate of her mother's chocolate chip cookies.

"Again my hero," Delaney told him with a smile.

"It's all Jeanne Marie." He set the tray on the coffee table and held out the glass. "Would you be more comfortable with your mother taking care of you? I can let her take over if that's what you want."

You're what I want, Delaney thought to herself, but answered, "This is fine." She tried to take the water from him, but his fingers remained curled around hers as he tipped the glass to her mouth. The water was refreshing and cooled her parched throat. As she pulled away, Cisco traced his thumb across her bottom lip, capturing a droplet of water. Delaney coughed as she swallowed, so shocked by the intimacy of his touch.

"Sorry," he said with a sheepish smile as he patted her between the shoulders. "I shouldn't distract you."

"You can distract me all you want," she answered, "especially when you try to get the boot off my foot."

His gaze turned serious. He pulled out a small utility knife from his back pocket. "We're going to need to sacrifice the boot for the greater good."

Delaney let out a halfhearted whimper. "I love these boots."

"I wish there were another way," Cisco told her, shaking his head. "But your ankle is too swollen."

"I know," she whispered, embarrassed when a few errant tears slipped from her eyes. "I can't believe I'm crying over a pair of cowboy boots. You must think I'm so silly."

"I think you're one of the strongest women I know," Cisco told her, bending forward to place his lips against the moisture on her cheek. He smoothed his hands through her hair, and she leaned into his strength. "I should have been there with you."

"It's okay," she told him again. "You're here now."

After a few moments he sat back, adjusting her foot to rest on his bent knee. Delaney tried not to notice the muscles that bunched under his jeans but failed miserably. As he took the knife to the perfectly worn leather, she figured it was better to focus on his body rather than how he was destroying her boot.

Her eyes drifted to his face, his focus laser sharp on his task. She felt the pressure around her injured ankle lessen and a moment later he held up the mangled boot for her inspection. "Sorry," he repeated.

She smiled wanly. "I'll miss them, but it feels better already."

He pulled off her sock and Delaney peeked at her foot, which looked small and pale cradled in his large tanned hands. Her ankle had swelled to nearly twice its normal size, the skin already bruised with a mix of dark blue and black. Cisco took the bag of ice and, after draping a washcloth over her ankle, placed the ice on top.

Delaney winced, then shivered but after a moment the coldness seeped through and began to soothe her ankle.

"The sprain isn't too bad," he told her, adjusting the bag. "I've sprained my ankle a few times playing basketball. You should feel better within a few days."

"Thank you for taking care of me."

"My pleasure." He dipped one of the washcloths into a bowl of water she hadn't noticed earlier on the tray and drew her arm out straight to dab at the scratch on its underside. "I wish I could do more."

His dark gaze captured hers and suddenly, despite her

exhaustion and the aches in her body, an electric energy charged the air between them. *You could kiss me.* The words popped into Delaney's mind and color flooded her cheeks. She was pretty sure Cisco could read her thoughts, as she saw his breathing go shallow.

At that moment her mother cleared her throat behind them. "I have the bandages and first-aid kit, if you're ready for them."

Cisco stood quickly, breaking their connection. "I should go so you can rest."

Delaney tried to hide her disappointment. It wasn't as if he didn't have more important things to do in his day than play nursemaid to her.

"I'd love to stay with you, but from here I'll just be in the way." He bent forward and kissed the top of her head, the first outward display of affection in front of someone in her family. Delaney took it as a positive sign of his attentions toward her. "I need to take care of a few things at the office—"

"Don't forget your meeting," she supplied, hoping she didn't sound peevish.

His gaze went gentle as he perched on the edge of the sofa next to her. "If you want me to stay, I will."

"And the meeting?"

"It can be rescheduled. I meant what I said, Delaney. You're my priority."

The sincerity in his eyes overwhelmed her. Delaney knew how important business was to Cisco and the fact that he'd choose her over his professional obligations made her heart pound. It also gave her the strength to let him go. "It's okay. Take care of your job. I'm in good hands here."

She glanced at her mother, who gave her an approving nod.

"Are you sure?" Cisco looked almost reluctant to leave. When she nodded, he straightened again. "I'll come by later to check on you after you rest. Unless you're too tired then—"

"I won't be too tired," she assured him.

"Thank you, Cisco." Her mother wrapped Cisco in one of her famous nurturing hugs.

Delaney smiled a little as she saw Cisco's strong shoulders visibly relax. Jeanne Marie's quiet, motherly way had that effect on everyone around her.

Cisco nodded at Jeanne Marie. "Let me know if she needs anything."

"We'll be fine."

"Rest," he said to Delaney. He looked as if there was more he wanted to add but glanced at her mother.

"I'll see you soon," Delaney told him, and he walked out with her mother.

Jeanne Marie returned a few minutes later.

"Are you sure you're okay?" She lifted the bag of ice to examine Delaney's foot. "It doesn't look too bad."

"The swelling is already going down. I'd like to shower, then rest for a bit. I think if I give it a little time, I should feel much better by tonight."

"Then let's get you upstairs." Her mother moved the coffee table to clear a path and helped Delaney stand. "You and Cisco are growing closer."

Delaney nodded. "I...really like him." She wasn't ready to admit the depth of her feelings to her mother.

"I can tell he cares about you."

"I think so, too, Mama." Despite the pain and fatigue, Delaney's heart sang. In her mind, one good thing had come out of this horrible day. She was certain that Cisco felt as much for her as she did for him.

She had a pretty good idea of how she was going to handle what came next.

Chapter Thirteen

"What do you mean, Alden Moore isn't here?"

"There was an emergency at one of the other properties," Kent Stephens explained. "He had to take care of it personally."

Cisco ran his hand through his still-wet hair as he paced back and forth across Kent's office. He'd busted his tail to get to this meeting on time after stopping at his rental house to change and shower. His time on the ranch had left him dirty, dusty and rethinking his whole purpose in Horseback Hollow. Seeing Delaney injured and the lengths she'd gone to in order to protect the lost calf had only cemented Cisco's respect for her and the way of life she held so dear.

He truly believed Cowboy Country in general, and the condos specifically, would have a much better reception in town if they could enhance the design and theme to feel more authentic to the true cowboy spirit that so many locals embodied.

Taking a few deep breaths, he pulled out his laptop and flipped it open on the conference table. At least he could discuss his ideas with Kent, who might pave the way for Alden to be more receptive to the changes.

"I wanted to talk to you both about reworking the design of the condos and the overall Cowboy Country brand." He slid into a chair across from Kent and plugged in the cord to connect his computer to the screen at the far end of the table.

"We're not paying you to come up with branding ideas." Kent shook his head. "You were hired to lock in the investors—"

"The guys in Lubbock are ready to sign," Cisco interrupted.

"—particularly the Fortunes," Kent finished. "So far all I've heard about on that front is you playing cowboy around town and sowing some Texas oats while you're at it."

Anger coursed through Cisco. He stood up, pressing his palms flat on the table to lean toward Kent. "What are you insinuating?"

"It's no secret you've gotten close with the youngest of Jeanne Marie Fortune Jones's kids. What's her name? Delilah?"

"Delaney," Cisco said through clenched teeth.

Kent leaned back in the chair, crossing his beefy arms over his chest. "I assume you're using her to secure your ties with the whole family. It's a decent strategy."

Cisco wanted to argue. Unfortunately, that was exactly how his relationship with Delaney had started. Now it was much more, but he didn't expect Kent to understand that. Hell, he barely understood it himself. In a matter of weeks, she'd become essential to his life. Making her happy was more important than any business deal that came his way.

"Leave the Fortunes out of the equation for a minute." He held up a hand when Kent began to speak. "Let me show you what I've done here." He powered on his computer and opened the presentation he'd prepared. He'd made the changes to the luxury condo development and highlighted the reasons behind them to appeal to Alden Moore directly. He hoped that Kent was forward thinking enough to consider this new proposal.

As he spoke, Cisco became more certain that this plan could satisfy the goals of both Cowboy Country and Moore Entertainment while alleviating some of the concerns of the people in Horseback Hollow. Unfortunately, Kent reached forward midway through the presentation and snapped shut Cisco's laptop.

"This is all well and good, Mendoza, but it's *not* part of the plan."

Cisco felt a muscle twitch in his jaw. "Plans change."

"Not these." Kent pushed back from the table and went to stand before the window that looked out to the theme park. "You know there have been some challenges with this opening. We're fighting to keep on schedule and, more important, on budget. There is no room to deviate. We need to get this place open and those condos built before public sentiment turns any further against us. Jobs are on the line."

"Yours being one of them?" Cisco supplied.

Kent didn't answer directly but the grim set of his mouth told Cisco he'd guessed correctly. "I haven't spent the better part of my career working for Alden Moore to have this nothing cow town get the best of me. Bring the Fortunes to the table, or I'll find someone who will."

"Will you share the ideas I've given you with Mr. Moore?"

"No way." Kent shook his head. "I'm not telling Alden anything that would lead him to believe I have less than one hundred percent confidence in the Cowboy Country model." The man turned, squeezing his fingers around the back of his chair. "We're a lot alike, Cisco. We've both worked hard for our success. My career is everything to me, just like yours is to you."

"Not anymore," Cisco whispered.

"Don't be a fool. This development is the opportunity of a lifetime for you. You get the deal done on this and your future with Moore Entertainment is set. I can tell you there are plenty of plans for brand expansion in the works, and you're going to want to be a part of them." Kent flashed an acid smile as he walked back to the conference table. "Get the Fortunes to ante up so we can lock in this deal before the grand opening and you'll be the golden boy. I don't care what you do on your own time. If you want to mess around with that little piece of cowgirl—"

Cisco shot up from the table, grabbing Kent by the collar and spinning him around. Kent was a big guy and probably had a good thirty pounds on him. But anger fueled Cisco as he slammed the other man into the wall. "Don't *ever* speak about Delaney that way."

"Fine." Kent coughed several times, trying to pull Cisco's hands away from his throat. "Sorry I mentioned it. Just get this deal done so we can move on, okay?"

Giving a sharp nod, Cisco released the man. He never lost his temper like that. He wanted to turn his back on

Cowboy Country right now, to walk away so that he could start fresh with Delaney. So that he could be the man she believed him to be, the man she deserved.

But he'd made a commitment to Moore Entertainment, and he'd never failed at a job before. He still believed he could make this right, but he'd have to come clean with Delaney on the entire situation first.

"I'll have it wrapped up by the end of the week," he told Kent as he packed up his laptop and the revised plans from the architect. "But I want to talk to Mr. Moore directly."

"I told you he's very busy, so—"

"If the Fortunes are so damn important, he'll make time."

Kent studied him for a moment, then nodded. "I'll check his calendar. If he's not going to be back in the office, I'll schedule a conference call."

"You know where to reach me." Cisco grabbed his bag and left the office without another word.

A gust of hot air hit him as he walked into the bright midday sun. He took a deep breath to clear his head. Of course Kent thought he was using Delaney. Normally Cisco wouldn't care. Other than his family, he'd allowed his personal life to fall by the wayside as he'd worked to achieve his professional goals.

Friends, and in particular girlfriends, had been just means to an end as he kept moving forward. He'd never taken the time to make the people around him and their needs a priority. He'd always believed he didn't need anyone, could handle anything life threw at him on his own. Now he saw how much that had cost him in life. More important, how much he stood to lose if he couldn't make Delaney understand his work with Cowboy Country.

He texted Delaney but didn't hear immediately back. He figured she might be resting, so, as much as he wanted to hear her voice, resisted the urge to follow up with a phone call. He walked around the theme park, taking in the brightly colored rides and carnival-type activities. Everything was shiny and new, but there was a distinct lack of activity within the park. Cisco knew there was dissension with the employees and Kent had alluded to even bigger problems. If the situation wasn't straightened out, it could have negative repercussions on not just the grand opening but the initial stages of the condo development, as well. But right now he was grateful for the quiet to regroup his thoughts.

After leaving Cowboy Country, he drove out to the condo site, imagining how the landscape would change once the housing development was built. He wondered how his life would look right now if he'd taken the time to consider how the deals he'd brokered over the years would impact the communities where they were built.

Hindsight might be twenty-twenty, but Cisco had never been a fan of dwelling in the past. He checked his phone but there was still no communication from Delaney. He decided to return to the rental house, change clothes from the meeting and call out to the ranch. It didn't matter if he had to sit at the foot of Delaney's bed and watch her sleep. Cisco had an overwhelming need to see her, to make sure she was still okay from the morning's turmoil, then figure out how to tell her everything that had happened with him.

As he drove across town to his house, he rehearsed several scenarios for explaining the whole truth of his job to her. The street was empty as he pulled into the driveway. The more he thought about seeing Delaney, of just being close to her, the more anxious he became to get to the ranch.

He fiddled with the front door lock—then realized the door wasn't locked. Although it probably didn't matter in a town like Horseback Hollow, Cisco hadn't gotten out of the big-city habit of locking everything up tight. It put him a little on edge as he walked through, but the sight that greeted him made him take a step back.

Candles were lit all around the living room, the shades partially drawn so that the flickering lights were the only thing that illuminated the space. That was surprise enough but what rocked him to his core was Delaney.

She stood in the middle of the room wearing nothing but a pale blue silk nightgown that barely grazed her thighs. A nervous smile curved her lips.

Cisco swallowed and opened his mouth to speak but found he was unable to produce even a single word.

Goose bumps pricked the back of Delaney's neck as Cisco continued to stare at her. Maybe it was just a few moments of shocked silence, but it felt like hours. She dug her fingernails into the flesh below the hem of her nightgown, feeling like the biggest fool in the world.

"Um…maybe this is a bad time," she stammered, itching to bolt through the house out the back door. "I should just go and—"

"No." The force in his tone kept her rooted where she stood. He held up a hand. "I… Give me a minute to…" He swiped his hand over his face. "Delaney, what are you doing out of bed?"

"The idea was sort of to get *into* bed," she said on a nervous rush of breath. Color flooded her cheeks and she bit down on her lip. "I didn't mean to say that out loud."

Even as his mouth kicked up, those brown eyes that did funny things to her belly turned smoky black. "I thought you were resting at home. Because of your ankle." He pointed to her feet but his gaze seemed to snag on her bare legs.

"Well, I took a couple of ibuprofen and a nap." She pulled her nightgown down to cover more of her legs, then realized she'd exposed most of her chest in the process.

The silk gown was held up by thin straps that tied in a delicate bow above each shoulder. She'd bought it on a whim almost six months ago when she'd been shopping with her sister in Vicker's Corners. At the time, Delaney hadn't had any idea of when she might wear it. But she'd woken up this afternoon feeling better physically but still so full of emotions from her ordeal with the baby calf and the fact that Cisco had been the one to find her. She believed with all her heart that he just needed a little push to reveal his feelings for her.

"I thought... I wanted to thank you for your help this morning," she stammered.

"You don't need to thank me, Delaney." His gaze was infinitely gentle. "Not like this."

Oh, no. This was her greatest fear come true. She'd put herself out there for this man, and he didn't want her. Blood roared in her ears as humiliation washed over her. If only the floor would open and swallow her whole. Since that was unlikely, Delaney did the next best thing. She turned and started to run for the back of the house. She'd parked her truck on the street behind Cisco's to make sure she surprised him.

Instead she was the one who was surprised. And mortified.

Her ankle slowed her down, and just as she got to the edge of the sofa, Cisco's hand wrapped around her upper arm. "Wait, Delaney, please. You don't understand."

"I think I do," she said, and tried to wrench free, but he held her fast. "It was a stupid idea and I'm just a dumb girl from a tiny Texas town. Nothing like the kind of woman you'd want—"

He spun her to face him. "You're exactly the kind of woman I'd want. The *only* woman I want."

Delaney seemed to relax at his words, so Cisco loosened his grip on her arm. He'd used more self-restraint in the past five minutes than he'd needed in his life to date.

"You mean that?" Delaney's big blue eyes still held a trace of doubt as she looked up at him.

"Of course I do." He lowered his head and kissed her bare shoulder. Her skin was impossibly soft and she smelled both sweet and sexy. Another wave of desire flooded through him, almost robbing him of speech once again. "You bring me to my knees. But I want to be worthy of you, Delaney. You deserve so much that—"

She wound her arms around his neck and pressed her mouth to his. "I want you, Cisco," she said against his lips. He forgot everything else as she tentatively stroked her tongue inside his mouth. Every part of her wound through his senses. His hands moved along the soft silk of her nightgown but it wasn't enough. He wanted to feel her skin against his.

The passion in their kiss exploded and it was all he could do to keep control of his need. He had so much to tell her, but right now there were no more words.

He scooped her into his arms, careful of her wrapped ankle as he moved through the house to his bedroom.

Flipping back the comforter, he laid her gently onto the bed, his heart constricting as he gazed down at her.

"This is what you want?" he asked, wanting the decision to be hers.

"More than anything," she answered, and reached for him.

He stood at the edge of the bed, loosening his tie as he did. Delaney helped him with the buttons of his shirt and he shucked it off, kicking off his boots at the same time. When he caught her gaze, hesitation flashed in her eyes. "What is it?" He lowered himself next to her. "If you're having second thoughts…"

"This is the first time I've seen you without a shirt," she answered. "Your body is… You're perfect. I don't want to disappoint you."

"I'm honored and so lucky to have you here with me." Slowly he traced one finger up her arm and hooked it under the strap of her nightgown. He tugged it off her shoulder, exposing the soft swell of her breast. "Nothing about you could disappoint me, Delaney. Tell me what you want. I want this night to be perfect for you. For us."

"I want to touch you," she whispered.

He moved closer as she sat up. Her palms were cool on his heated flesh as she ran them along his shoulders, then down his chest. He could see her chest rise and fall in shallow breaths. He practically groaned when her fingers grazed his nipple. Her touch was innocent and seductive at the same time. Cisco had never been so aroused by a woman. He watched her face as her hands moved down his stomach to the waistband of his dress slacks. "You're still wearing too many clothes."

He barked out a chuckle. "Minx," he whispered, but stood again. He undid his pants and pushed them to the ground. Even through his boxers, he knew there'd be no hiding how much he wanted her. The fact that her tongue darted out to unconsciously lick her bottom lip forced all the breath to hiss out of his lungs.

All he could think was that he had this moment to treasure her, to show her all the ways she meant so much to him. "I'm going to worship every inch of you."

As he bent over the bed once more, her eyes clouded. "I'm still not sure I can measure up to what you're used to. I don't want you to compare me—"

He placed a finger over her lips. "There is no comparison to you, Delaney." He wasn't sure where her worry came from when she was so confident in her life and who she was. How could she not realize she was perfect to him? Had some other man in her past caused her to doubt herself? The flickering thought made him want to hunt down the idiot. But right now his only priority was helping her to understand that every part of this night would be special to him. "Making love is like dancing—you need the right partner to make it good."

She studied him for a moment, and then her lips curved into a sexy smile. "We were pretty good dancing together."

"The best," he confirmed.

It was as if a switch had been thrown inside her. Her eyes lit with desire again and she laced her fingers behind his neck, drawing him to her. His mouth slanted over hers and the kiss turned immediately intense, hot and something more. She moved underneath him and he trailed kisses along her jaw in response, balancing with his hands on either side of her body as he moved his attentions down her neck and then lower, peeling the delicate nightgown off her as he went. He licked one breast, circling the sensitive peak, and was rewarded with a soft moan of pleasure from her. He divided his attention between the two, his touch both gentle and demanding.

She breathed his name, and it was the most beautiful sound in the world.

He moved lower, pulling the silk all the way off her body, nearly losing his control when he realized she wore nothing underneath. The fabric of her nightgown caught on the bandage that wrapped her ankle, reminding him what she'd been through today. What he'd been unable to control and how much the thought of Delaney in jeopardy had terrified him. He ran his hands down her leg, then lifted the injured foot and gently kissed the arch.

"I will never let anything hurt you, *cielo*." He ran his tongue along the back of her calf. She wiggled as he got closer to her knee. "A new discovery," he said with a smile. "You're ticklish."

"And I'm still more naked than you."

At that he laughed. "Is it possible to be *more* naked?"

"You know what I mean," she said, then gasped as his teeth grazed the inside of her thigh. "Cisco!"

"Yes, Delaney?" His voice hummed against her skin and he felt her shiver.

"Take your boxers off."

He nipped at her, then raised himself up, removing his boxers as quickly as he could.

As he lowered himself over her again, his gaze tracked to her face. He expected her to still be watching him, but instead her eyes were squeezed shut, the tension on her face pulling at his heart. Some guy had done a real number on her. Cisco settled himself next to her, propped on one elbow, his fingers tracing a slow path along her belly. "Open your eyes, sweetheart."

One blue iris squinted at him. "It's good," she whispered. "It's all good."

"Are you trying to convince yourself or me?"

She opened her other eye. "Both."

"We are going to be better than good, Delaney. This is going to be perfect. For you. For me. Together."

She gave a jerky nod and opened for him as he kissed her. As the kiss deepened, he let his fingers explore lower until he brushed her warm center. She whimpered and he caught the sound in his mouth, levering himself over her as he continued to touch her, the rhythm becoming faster as she finally relaxed enough to let pleasure take control of her body. Her fingernails grazed his back as she pulled him tighter, then broke apart in his arms, crying out his name.

"I need you so much, Delaney," he told her as he grabbed a foil packet from the nightstand drawer. "I need to be inside you."

"Yes," she whispered, her eyes still glazed. She lifted her head and kissed him again, nearly pushing him over the edge.

He'd known her for weeks, wanted her almost immediately and felt as though he'd needed her for his entire life. Understanding that this moment would change what was between them, he drove into her, needing to be enveloped in her. But only when her eyes flew open, pain flashing in their blue depths, did he truly understand how much things had changed.

Chapter Fourteen

"Delaney..." Cisco spoke her name on a harsh breath. She felt him begin to pull away but had no intention of allowing her first time to end before it even got started. She wrapped her arms more tightly around him, pressing herself against him.

"Don't stop," she whispered, and he moved again, his whole body rigid from his attempt to keep the motion gentle.

As the initial pain eased, pressure began to build inside her once more. Similar to when he touched her but deeper, as if her whole body were on fire. She raked her fingers through his hair and whispered into his ear, "More, Cisco. Now." Then she sucked his earlobe into her mouth, grazing his skin with her teeth in a move she'd learned from him minutes before.

He groaned and increased his speed, hooking his hand

around her leg, holding it in a way that made her understand he was trying to protect her injured ankle. The fact that he was still trying to take care of her, keeping his own passion in check for her, only made her more frenzied.

She moved against him, telling him with her body what she wanted. She felt herself about to fall over the edge and clung to him with every ounce of strength she had. "I love this," she told him, the words as ragged as her breathing.

"I love you," he whispered in response, and that was all it took to drive her the rest of the way. She shattered and every fireworks display she'd ever seen seemed to go off in her mind at the same time. She felt him shudder before going still against her. His breath was warm against her neck and eventually it steadied to the same pace as hers.

He slipped out of her, tenderly kissing the hollow of her throat. He lifted onto his forearms, then used his fingers to spread her hair across the pillow. She watched him but he seemed completely focused on his gentle ministrations. It was a shock when his gaze slammed into hers. There were so many emotions swirling in his dark eyes. She couldn't begin to read them all.

"Surprise," she whispered.

"Delaney. *Cielo.*" He pressed his forehead to hers, then lifted again, studying her. "Why didn't you tell me?"

"That I was a virgin?" She rolled her eyes. "It's not something that lends itself to casual conversation."

"How about serious conversation? I've told you before that you are precious to me. What you gave me tonight is a gift, sweetheart. If I'd known…"

"If you'd known, you probably wouldn't have made

love to me, Cisco. Beneath that polished get-the-deal-done exterior, you are a gentleman."

He shook his head. "I could have made it better for you."

"Since it was perfect, that's highly unlikely." She drew him to her for a slow kiss. "But you're welcome to try. I just hope it was good enough for you…that you aren't disappointed since—"

He lifted one hand to cup her face and eased his thumb back and forth across her cheek. "That was the most powerful experience I've ever had, Delaney. I'm not exactly a novice, but I didn't know it could be like that."

She released a breath. The fact that he'd been as affected as she was gave her the confidence to continue. "What you said…during… I know sometimes things get blurted out in the heat of passion. It's okay if you didn't really mean it. I understand."

"I love you." His gaze never wavered from hers as he spoke the words. "That may have been the first time I said it, but it certainly won't be the last. I intend to be a part of your life for a long time, Delaney Fortune Jones. You are mine now."

She pushed him to his back and leaned over him, letting her long hair cover them both. "That goes both ways, Cisco Mendoza. You are mine right back. There is no one else, no one I want to share this experience or my life with other than you."

He kissed her, running his hands up and down her body, and desire flared in her again. Unfortunately, the moment was somewhat ruined by a loud growl from her stomach.

"Ignore that," she told him.

Cisco laughed, easing her head away from his. "Are

you kidding? I've heard stories about you. From what your family says, you and hunger aren't a good combination."

"True," she admitted. "But I bet you could keep me happy."

"I'm going to make you happy." He turned her onto her back again but slid out of the bed before she could stop him. "I'm also going to keep you well fed."

As if it understood his words, her belly rumbled again. "Probably a smart idea." She sat up as he turned and pulled on his boxer shorts. The back view of Cisco was just as yummy as the front.

He glanced over his shoulder. "I can feel you ogling me."

"You have to admit I'm one smart cowgirl. When I decided you would be my first, it helped to know you were easy on the eyes."

With a laugh, Cisco clutched at his chest. "Should I feel taken advantage of?"

Delaney waited until his eyes met hers to speak. "I would never use you, Cisco. That isn't how love looks where I come from."

For an instant a shadow crossed his face. Then he leaned down and took her mouth in a slow, sensual kiss. "Right now I want you to stay put. Let me take care of you."

"How can I argue with a request like that?"

When he disappeared into the bathroom, Delaney let her eyes drift shut. Her body was a little sore, but she mostly felt happy and satisfied. The way Cisco looked at her when he told her he loved her made her feel certain she wasn't just another notch on his belt. They had something real, and Delaney couldn't wait to start building their life together.

She could hear water running as Cisco returned to the bedroom. "How do you feel about a hot bath while I heat up dinner?"

"You ran a bath for me?" Pulling the sheet around her, Delaney scooted to the edge of the bed. "Seriously, Mendoza, you have to stop being so perfect."

He'd put on a T-shirt and a pair of athletic shorts over his boxers. "My goal is your total satisfaction," he said with a wink.

"I can live with that." She stood and moved toward the bathroom, stopping to give him a kiss as she passed.

"Do you need help with your ankle?"

She shook her head. "I've got it."

The bathtub was oversized and after unwrapping her ankle, she sank into the warm water, quickly washing before turning off the tap. Steam rose and her tired muscles appreciated the soaking. Normally she could spend a long time relaxing in the bath, but tonight all she wanted was to be near Cisco again. She dried off and rewrapped the bandage, then noticed the robe Cisco had left for her draped over the sink. She inhaled the scent of him as she slipped into the thick cotton, then padded to the kitchen.

He was at the stove, his back turned to her. She watched him in silence for several minutes, enjoying the easy way he moved. He looked as comfortable in the kitchen as he'd become on the ranch. She could imagine he fit in just as well in a boardroom. He flicked off the burner and turned, grinning as he noticed her.

"You look good in my robe."

"I feel good in it, too."

He motioned to a tall seat at the island with his elbow.

"Have a seat. I've got plans for you later and want to make sure you keep up your strength."

She laughed and climbed into the chair. "Wicked plans?"

"Always." He set a bowl on the counter in front of her. "It's a simple pasta recipe."

"Carbs," she said on a contented sigh. "My favorite."

Cisco uncorked a bottle of wine and poured them each a glass, then came to sit next to her. "To us," he said, raising his glass to hers.

"To our future." She took a sip of wine, cool and crisp on her tongue, then picked up her fork. "This smells amazing." It was a penne pasta with a light sauce of olive oil, mushrooms, garlic and spices. "And tastes even better," she told him after taking a bite.

"I aim to please."

Which could be the understatement of the century as far as Delaney was concerned. They talked and laughed as they ate. It gave Delaney great comfort that as physically attracted as she was to Cisco, their connection was much deeper than that. He was a friend, someone she wanted to share the details of her day with and hear about his from. It still bothered her that he hadn't shared everything about his business in Horseback Hollow, but that was bound to change now that they'd taken the next step in their relationship.

Being with a man wasn't a decision Delaney had made lightly, but she knew she'd picked the right partner with Cisco for many reasons.

As they cleared the dishes into the sink, he glanced at the clock on the stove. "It's getting late. Do you need to call your parents? I wouldn't want them to worry."

She shook her head. "I told my mom I was spending the night at my sister's and asked Stacey to cover for me."

"You shouldn't have to deceive your parents for me."

"It's not like that. I'm an adult. They respect that…sort of." She shrugged. "But I live at home and that makes things complicated. I was nervous enough coming over here." She flashed a smile. "The added stress of worrying about what my parents might think didn't seem like a great idea."

He took the wineglass from her hands, set it on the table and wrapped his fingers around hers. "So you came here for the express purpose of seducing me?"

"Did the candles and nightgown give it away?"

He tipped back his head and laughed. "How did I get so lucky?"

She squeezed his hand. "I have no idea. You're arrogant, a player, a know-it-all, way too confident…"

"And your perfect match?" he suggested.

"So it would seem."

"Are you finished seducing me, Delaney?"

She bit down on her bottom lip, watching his eyes darken in response. "I've barely gotten started."

Cisco bent forward and picked her up, once again loving how tiny she felt in his arms. As spirited and independent as Delaney was, there had been a lot of risk in coming to him today. She'd put aside her pride and allowed herself to be vulnerable for him.

He knew things weren't going to always be this easy, especially since he still owed her an explanation for why he'd sought her out in the first place. But that was a conversation for the morning. Tonight he wanted only to show her how much she meant to him, to make sure the memory of her first night would always be perfect.

"Did you put clean sheets on the bed while I was in the bath?" Delaney asked as he walked into the bedroom with her.

"I cook *and* do laundry," he said, setting her on her feet next to the bed. "I think that makes me quite a catch." He tugged on the belt of the robe. "You'd better not let me go."

"I'm definitely not letting you go."

He slid his hands inside her robe, watching as she hitched in a breath. The robe fell from her shoulders and she was perfect standing in front of him, her skin flushed and soft to the touch.

"Oh, no," she whispered, lifting the hem of his T-shirt. "I'm not going to be undressed alone. We're in this together."

There was nothing he wanted more at this moment than to be joined with this woman, skin to skin. The shirt dropped to the ground along with his boxers and the two of them fell to the bed, kissing and exploring each other. Delaney's hesitation from earlier was gone. She was all innocent curiosity and confidence. It drove him crazy in the best way possible.

But he wanted to savor every moment with her, so deliberately slowed their pace. As if sensing what he wanted, Delaney did the same. They took their time, whispering endearments to each other as the fire between them built again, even more intense than before. When he finally entered her, Cisco could barely speak.

"I love you," he managed to whisper, and she tightened her hold on him. She couldn't know how much it meant to him to say those words. He hadn't even realized how long he'd been waiting to find her. But when they fell over the edge together, he had no doubt that he'd spend the rest of his life trying to make Delaney as happy as she made him.

So when he woke up the next morning alone, Cisco wasn't immediately worried. After making love, they'd stayed awake talking for most of the night. He'd finally drifted to sleep with her wrapped in his arms. He usually set the alarm on his smartphone for 6:00 a.m., but the clock on the nightstand showed that it was almost seven thirty. His phone wasn't where he'd plugged it in to charge and neither was Delaney's. He got out of bed, pulled on a pair of shorts over his boxers and headed to the kitchen.

He hoped she wasn't bothering with making breakfast. He was still worried about her resting her ankle and wanted to take care of her as much as he could until she was back to normal.

The house was empty and eerily quiet as he came out from the bedroom. "Delaney?" he called, but silence was the only answer.

Glancing out the front window, a flash of unease skittered down his back when he realized her truck wasn't in the driveway, where he'd moved it to late last night. He kept walking toward the kitchen, where a carton of eggs and jug of milk sat out, as if Delaney had been interrupted in the middle of pulling food from the fridge. What the hell had happened and where was she? His gaze stopped on a piece of notebook paper that sat on the counter, his cell phone placed on top of it.

He read the words printed in Delaney's delicate handwriting. *"Your boss texted. He wants an update on when you're going to 'close the Fortunes.' You should have plenty to tell him after last night."*

His heart dropped as he picked up his phone and hit a few buttons to review the text that had come in early this morning. Damn. He wasn't sure how or why Delaney had seen that text, but it didn't matter. All he cared about was making her understand that there was more to the story—more to *him*—than she clearly thought.

Punching in her number, he hurried back to the bedroom and threw on a shirt and slid his feet into running shoes. The phone clicked immediately to Delaney's voice mail. Cisco muttered a curse, then left a message, asking her to call him back, that he could explain what she'd seen. He needed her to give him a chance and didn't care that he sounded as if he was begging.

He'd get down on his knees if that was what it took to make things right with Delaney.

He grabbed his keys from the kitchen counter, then ran to his truck and headed out toward the Fortune Jones family ranch. The phone rang when he was halfway there and he picked it up before looking at the display.

"Where are you?" he blurted. "You have to let me see you."

There was a pause at the other end of the line. Then Kent Stephens's deep voice answered. "The better question is where the hell are *you*, Mendoza? Did you get my texts this morning? Alden is here in the office and he wants to meet with you. Now."

"Can't do it." Cisco turned onto the county highway that led to the ranch and hit the gas pedal hard. He put the phone on speaker so he could concentrate on driving.

"You don't have a choice," Kent practically yelled. Cisco heard him take a breath and his next words were at a more normal pitch. "He wants an answer on the Fortunes. We need the meeting set up with the family ASAP."

"No Fortunes," Cisco shot back. "That part of the deal is off the table." He started down the driveway that led to the ranch, tension radiating through him.

"Are you kidding? Alden is going to—"

"Gotta go, Kent." Cisco parked in front of the house and turned off the ignition. "We'll make this thing go without the Fortunes or not at all."

"Listen to me, Men—"

"I'll call you later." Cisco ended the call and pocketed the phone as he jumped out of the truck. He ran up the steps and rang the doorbell twice, bouncing on the balls of his feet as he waited for someone to answer. He was ready to figure out which bedroom window was Delaney's and climb up to her Romeo-style if he got that desperate.

It didn't come to that when a moment later the door opened. Jeanne Marie smiled at him. "Cisco, what a lovely surprise."

He tried to keep his face neutral, shocked that he was still getting such a warm welcome from Delaney's mother. "Could I speak to Delaney?"

A frown creased Jeanne Marie's brow. "I'm sorry—she's not here this morning. She spent the night at her sister's house, so she's probably still there. You didn't know?"

"Uh…I guess…I haven't been able to reach her this morning."

She reached out and patted his arm. "Is everything all right, Cisco?"

He scrubbed his hands across his face, unsure how

to answer. He didn't want to reveal too much to Jeanne Marie if Delaney hadn't talked to her yet. How did you explain to a mother that you'd taken her daughter's innocence and betrayed her in the same twelve-hour time stretch? Not a great way to endear himself to his girlfriend's family.

Was it safe to call Delaney his girlfriend after this morning? He couldn't very well call her anything if she wouldn't speak to him.

"If you talk to her, would you please tell her I stopped by?" He cleared his throat and added another "Please." He met Jeanne Marie's kind gaze. "I care about your daughter very much. No matter what happens, I hope you know that."

"Of course you do. She's never opened herself up to someone like she has with you, Cisco. Delaney is special to all of us in the family. She's supported her sister and brothers as they've found love and deserves to be happy in her own life, too. I believe she could find that happiness with you."

Cisco took a step back then locked his knees so they wouldn't buckle. In her gentle way, this sweet, well-meaning woman had run him down harder than a two-ton bull. "Thank you, Mrs. Fortune Jones. Delaney deserves the world, and I'm going to be the man to give it to her."

He returned to his truck and drove, slowly now, down the driveway and back onto the highway. After a few minutes, he pulled over, unsure which way to go. He called Delaney and again went to voice mail. He left another message, then texted her for good measure.

Jeanne Marie's words reverberated in his head. Delaney *could* find happiness with him. What had happened between them was a misunderstanding. Yes, he should have told her sooner, but once he explained it, she'd see why he'd waited. Then there was the issue of Cowboy Country and making the deal go through without the support of the Fortunes. Cisco would just have to convince Alden Moore of how the condo development could work and why the changes he was suggesting would benefit everyone in the end.

His phone rang and he grabbed it off the seat, disappointed when Matteo's name showed up on the display. He answered anyway, hoping maybe Delaney had turned to Rachel for support after leaving his house this morning. Cisco had to find a way to track her down.

"Hey, Matteo."

"What's wrong?"

"How do you know something's wrong?"

"You sound like someone just kicked your puppy."

"I don't have a dog."

Matteo chuckled. "You know what I mean."

Cisco wrapped the fingers of his free hand around the steering wheel. He hated asking for help but had little choice right now. "Any chance Rachel's talked to Delaney today?"

"Doubt it. We've been together all morning. Why?"

"I'm trying to track her down and having trouble reaching her."

"You've called?"

"Yes."

"And texted?"

"Matteo," Cisco said in a warning voice. "I'm familiar with how to contact a person. That's not the problem."

"So when you say 'trouble,' what you mean is you're in trouble with the girl."

Cisco sighed. There was no point in hiding what had

happened to his brother. Horseback Hollow was small enough that Matteo would find out eventually. "She's really mad and won't take my calls. I messed up and am scared as hell that I've ruined my chances with her. I've been to her parents', but she's not there. I don't know what else to do, bro. I'm desperate here."

Silence filled the line and then Matteo burst out laughing. "Scared? Desperate? Did I just hear those two words from the unbeatable Cisco Mendoza? My brother knocked off his game by love. I never thought I'd live to see the day."

"Come on, man. I'm serious."

"What happened? Did you flirt with another woman? Call her the wrong name?"

"Don't be a jerk. I care about Delaney. I…" He paused, then said, "I think I'm in love with her."

He heard Matteo whistle. "That's a big deal for you."

"No kidding. But there's a business deal I've been working on and it involves Cowboy Country." He rested his head on the seatback. "And the Fortunes."

"The Fortunes aren't known to be fans of the theme park. From what Gabi says, most of them have been against it from the start. All except…"

"Delaney," Cisco finished for him. "There were things I didn't tell her. Details I should have shared and now it might be too late."

"You'll be fine, Cisco."

"What makes you so sure?"

"Because you're a master negotiator, king of the close. Hell, you could sell snow to an Eskimo. Delaney doesn't stand a chance against your skills."

"It's different with her."

"No way. All deals work the same way and I've never

seen you fail once you put your mind to something. Give her some time to cool off, then work your magic. She'll see—" The line beeped, cutting off the rest of Matteo's words. "I need to take that call," his brother said a moment later.

"Sure thing." Cisco sighed. "Thanks for listening."

"My pleasure, believe me. Let me know how things go once you track her down."

His brother clicked off the line and Cisco tossed the phone onto the seat. Two months ago he would have taken Matteo's words as a compliment. He prided himself on the career he'd built, making money and his professional reputation. He was a master at convincing people to do what he wanted, both in his work and his personal life. But Delaney *was* different. She'd seen more in him and he'd wanted to be that man for her. He'd make things right between them, but not because he could manipulate her into forgiving him. He had to make her see that he'd meant it when he told her he loved her.

Suddenly he had an idea of where she might be. He called his sister for directions, then turned the truck around on the highway until he could pull off at the road that led to the small ranch house Stacey shared with her husband, Colton, and her daughter, Piper.

It made sense that Delaney would first go to her sister's instead of back to her parents' house since that was where she'd supposedly spent the night. His heart jumped when he saw Delaney's truck parked next to the cozy house.

The sun shone bright as he climbed the front steps of the house. It had been only hours, but it felt like days since he'd seen Delaney. He couldn't wait to be near her again, to make her understand and then wrap her in his arms and never let go.

The door to the house opened before he even knocked. Stacey stood in the threshold, hands on her small hips. He'd met Stacey at the family barbecue but hadn't talked long to her. Now she held out her hand, palm facing him. "Don't come any closer."

He stopped at the edge of the top step.

"You might as well turn right around, Cisco. There isn't anything for you here."

It was no surprise that Stacey was standing sentry, guarding her little sister. But Cisco was on a mission and nothing was going to stop him.

"I'm not leaving until I see her." A breeze kicked up, and he could have sworn Delaney's sweet, flowery perfume floated around him on the air. His heart squeezed in response to her scent. "I hurt her, and you have no idea how sorry I am for that. I need a chance to make it right." He eased forward, his gaze never wavering from Stacey's. He had to make her see how important this was to him.

She shifted, crossing her arms over her chest, as if weighing his words against her protective instinct toward Delaney. "Don't think because she's strong and feisty that you can't break her heart. She's got a delicate soul and she needs someone who will take care of her, not toss her aside when the next shiny penny comes along."

"I would never—"

"Or use her as a pawn to further his career," she interrupted.

The words hit as intended, but Cisco wasn't going to give up so easily. "I made a mistake. I'm here to make things right. I have to talk to her, Stacey."

She bit down on her lip, the gesture so similar to Delaney's. It reminded Cisco that Delaney had a whole tribe of people surrounding her, ready to fight for her.

"No promises, but I'll see if she's available." Stacey turned on her heel and slammed the door in his face. A moment later it opened and she popped her head out. "Curse my mama for raising us with proper manners." She gestured for to him to follow. "Come on into the family room. I can't let you wait out here, even if you deserve it."

Cisco wasn't going to argue a foot in the door. "Thank you," he said, and followed her into the house.

She left him in a cozy family room off the kitchen. "Sit down and wait. If Delaney wants to see you, she'll come down. It's her choice, so don't follow me. Piper is napping, and if you wake her up, I really will have to kill you."

He shook his head. "I won't make a sound," he vowed. "And I'll wait for Delaney. It's her choice."

Still worrying her bottom lip, Stacey nodded, then disappeared.

Cisco lowered himself to the couch, determined to follow her directions to the letter. He checked the time on his smartphone and noticed that he'd missed several calls from Kent Stephens. He ignored the voice mails. There was nothing going on at Cowboy Country that couldn't wait until he worked things out with Delaney. His gaze was drawn to the shelves that flanked the fireplace in the comfortable room. Despite his promise to Stacey, he stood, drifting toward the bookcases. They were lined with family photos and mementos. He picked up a frame, a picture of a toddler he recognized as Stacey's daughter, Piper. Other photos showed Stacey, Colton and Piper together while others were pictures that included the ex-

tended Fortune Jones family. He traced Delaney's outline with his thumb, his heart constricting in a way he
barely understood.

Unfamiliar emotions rushing through him, he returned
the frame to its place on the shelf and glanced around the
room. The house looked new in its construction, but Stacey had decorated in a way that made it seem as though
they'd lived there for years. In addition to the family
photos, framed pictures of simple child art hung on the
walls along with colorful landscapes. A thick rug covered
the wide-plank wood floors, and two overstuffed chairs
flanked the sofa he'd been sitting on. One corner of the
room was taken over by neatly stacked children's toys.

This home was so different than the sleek lines and expensive leather that filled his condo back in Miami. He'd
always prided himself on having the best of everything—
appliances, electronics. His house was state-of-the-art
in every way, but now he realized it was also an empty
shell. He'd been filling his life with material things, but
they'd never made him truly happy. He thought back to
his childhood, traveling for his father's career in the air
force. His mother had made every place they lived feel
like home, much as Stacey's ranch house did.

This was what he wanted. The thought dawned on
him suddenly. It wasn't just Delaney and the chance to
have her fit into his world. He wanted to be a part of her
life, to build a future with her that included laughter and
tears, kids and pets underfoot. He wanted what his sister
and brother had found in Horseback Hollow. This town
could be home to him, too—as long as he had Delaney
by his side. All of the things he'd worked for—the money
and material success—now seemed so inconsequential in
comparison. Resolve filled him, along with a burgeon-

ing sense of excitement. It wasn't the adrenaline rush that came from brokering a big deal but the anticipation of finally having something real in his life—if Delaney would give him another chance. He could see it all in his mind, raising their family, growing old together.

A noise sounded behind him and he whirled around. He took an unconscious step forward, still caught up in his daydream, but the look on Delaney's face halted him in his tracks. She stood behind the couch, her arms crossed over her stomach. His whole body went still at the sight of her. He'd half expected her to come into the room, proverbial guns blazing, ready to put him in his place. At this point, he'd welcome her temper, raging anger—any display of emotion. Because at the moment her blue eyes were dull as they watched him, her beautiful face pale and expressionless. It was as if there was no life left inside her, that he'd snuffed it out by not trusting her enough to tell her the truth.

And despite all his dreams for their future, he realized he had no idea how to make things right between them again.

Chapter Fifteen

If it had been possible to reach in and pull her heart from her body, Delaney would have done it in that second. Because while she might be wrecked to her core by Cisco's betrayal, her heart still sped at the sight of him. Only now instead of just pleasure it was a mix of sweet memories—the way he'd touched her, the words he'd whispered—corrupted by the knowledge that he'd used her as a means to further his career.

"I would have helped you," she said quietly, fisting her hand and lifting it to rub against her chest as if she could ease the ache. "With all of it. The condos, the real estate deal, making inroads with my family…"

"It wasn't like that. Put together, it all seems much worse. That isn't how I meant for—"

"If only you'd told me the truth," she finished.

"I was going to," he offered quickly. "Last night. My

plan was to tell you all of it, every last detail." He ran his hands through his hair, clearly trying to figure out a way to make her understand. How could she ever understand? "Then you were at the house when I got there and…"

"I made a complete fool of myself?" Delaney shook her head. "I practically threw myself at you. I was so naive."

"No." He took a step, then seemed to hold himself back. "I was overwhelmed by everything…how beautiful you looked, how much I wanted you, my feelings, touching you—"

"Stop. Don't do that, Cisco. I won't be manipulated by you anymore than I already have."

"Is that what you think I did?"

"You should have told me from the beginning. You used me from the start."

"I'm sorry, Delaney. If I'd explained everything up front, before you knew me, would you really have agreed to any of it? You thought I was a player, a city slicker who couldn't understand everything this town stands for."

It was the truth—she'd thought all those things about him. "Apparently I was right."

"I do understand. Because of you. You taught me so much, Delaney. You changed me."

"The texts I saw this morning tells a different story. You know, I was trying to take care of you the way you had me. When your alarm went off and you didn't wake up, I took your phone to the kitchen to let you sleep. Then all of those messages came through one right after another. I thought there might be an emergency, so I looked at them." She shook her head. "Why do I even care that you don't think I was checking up on you?"

"You have full access to my phone, *cielo*. I'm sorry

you found out that way, but I don't want any more secrets between us."

"I'm not your *cielo*. I'm not your anything. Was seducing me part of the master plan for getting in good
with the Fortunes?"

His mouth dropped open and she watched as he sucked
in a breath as if her words had knocked the air from his
lungs. Good. She shouldn't be the only one in so much
pain.

"How can you think that? Yes, I wanted information
from you and I went about it the wrong way. But I would
never have slept with you for any reason other than the
feelings between us. You have to believe me, Delaney."

Oh, she wanted to. Her whole body ached, wrung out
from hours of crying and the stabbing pain of Cisco's de-
ception. She'd chosen him as her first, and he'd betrayed
her. Yet a small piece of her still yearned for him, for the
comfort and safety she'd felt in his arms. "Why should I?"

"I've already talked to the other executives at Cowboy
Country. They know the Fortunes are off the table. What
we had was real, Delaney. It *is* real. Nothing is more important to me than you."

"You told them there's no deal with the Fortunes?"

"I did more than that. I admitted I don't know most of
the Fortunes that well. And that the ones I do know, the
Horseback Hollow Fortunes, have valid concerns about
the theme park." He shook his head. "I've been trying
to meet with Alden Moore for over a week to show him
my ideas for adding more authenticity to the Cowboy
Country brand. I don't care if I lose my job over this. The
time I spent on your family's ranch meant a lot to me. I
learned what makes this community special, the values

the town holds dear. I want to honor that. I want to honor you. Give me another chance to prove it."

Her body swayed with need and she almost took a step forward. Who was she kidding? She very nearly threw herself across the room and into his embrace. She might be adventurous and occasionally impetuous, but the decision to make love to Cisco hadn't been a whim. She loved him with all her heart and, as much as she might want to, couldn't turn off those feelings so easily. Standing in front of her, waiting for an answer, he looked as awful as she felt. That was some small comfort.

But she couldn't trust him again so easily. What if this was simply more maneuvering? Her biggest fear about Cisco was that she wouldn't be enough for him. He loved a challenge and the thrill of the chase. What if she let him back in and he hurt her again? The stabbing pain in her heart this morning had been agonizing. She wasn't sure if she could take another round of that.

It was time to grow up. Delaney had little experience with men, but she knew herself very well. Their relationship had a chance only if she could truly put the pain he'd caused behind her. And she wasn't going to forgive him until she was certain she could trust him again.

"Thank you for trying to make this right, Cisco." She closed her eyes. "But I need more time." Her voice caught on the last word, her heart fighting against her mind's resolve.

"Delaney—"

She held up a hand. "I need time," she repeated, and turned to walk away.

"You'd better not get chocolate on my seat."

Delaney climbed into Galen's truck two days later, her

fingers wrapped tightly around her favorite candy bar. "I'm not a kid anymore, Galen. But just for fun I might smear a little along the dash."

"Not funny, Flapjack. Aren't we going to lunch at the Grill?"

She nodded, fastening the seat belt as he pulled out of the driveway. "Yes, I'm starving." She popped the last bite of chocolate into her mouth.

"But you just finished—" he took the wrapper from her hand, glanced at it, then dropped it in one of the cup holders between them "—a king-size bar of chocolate."

"That was an appetizer," she told him. "Don't judge. It's been a tough week."

"I thought a broken heart was supposed to kill your appetite."

"Who said my heart is broken?"

Galen gave her a sympathetic smile. "Do you want to talk about it?" he asked cautiously.

"You're the best brother ever." Delaney patted his arm, feeling emotion clog her throat. It was true she didn't have much appetite, but eating was the only thing that seemed to keep her tumbling emotions in check. "But right now I just want to have lunch and forget everything else. Okay?"

"Music to my ears." Galen's relief was obvious.

They drove in silence the rest of the way to town. Delaney kept her gaze on the scenery going by, although she could feel Galen look over at regular intervals. She appreciated the concern, but she couldn't take any more coddling. Her ankle had healed but she was still taking it easy, leaving her far too often in her parents' house.

Word of Cisco's betrayal had sped through the Fortune Joneses like a flash flood. Each member of her family seemed to be taking a turn with her, as if she might crumble if she was alone for too long.

That didn't seem a likely possibility and it barely surprised her to see Stacey waiting on the sidewalk in front of the Grill when they parked.

"What are you doing here?" Galen asked as the lock button on the truck beeped.

"Taking my sister to lunch," Stacey answered, wrapping an arm around Delaney's shoulders.

Galen held the door for Delaney and Stacey to enter the popular restaurant. "Then what am I doing here?"

"Picking up the tab," the sisters answered in unison.

"Glad I could be useful to the two of you."

The hostess seated them at a booth near the back and a waitress appeared within moments to take their orders.

"Have you talked to Cisco again since he came to the house?" Stacey asked when the three of them were alone.

Delaney shook her head at the same time Galen said, "You better not talk to him again." He pointed a finger at Delaney. "Ever again. I'd like to run that no-good city boy out of town."

"Galen, don't say that."

"It's true. If it wasn't for Gabi and Orlando, I'd have had words with Cisco already. Out of respect to the rest of the Mendozas, I'm letting it go. For now. But if I hear he's not leaving you alone, all bets are off."

"No need for the chest thumping, Galen." Stacey took a sip from the iced tea the waitress had brought her. "If Delaney wants to talk to Cisco, that's her choice."

"I hope you're not encouraging her…" Galen broke off as the waitress set three plates of food down in front of them. Out of habit, he handed Delaney the ketchup bottle first but kept his gaze on Stacey. "After what he did to her, that jerk should be strung up by his expensive loafers."

"He wears cowboy boots when he's helping on the ranch," Stacey countered. "And a hat just like yours."

Galen ran a finger over the brim of his cowboy hat, then picked up a fry. "Just because he dresses the part doesn't mean he has the first clue about life in Horseback Hollow. Or what it takes to make Delaney happy."

Delaney opened her mouth to tell her siblings what would make her happy, but Stacey spoke first.

"You didn't see him when he came to the house." Stacey cut her hamburger in half as she spoke. "He made a mistake, a big one. But he's genuinely sorry and wants to make it right. I think she should give him a chance."

"I think you're crazy."

Finally, Delaney'd had enough of their bickering. She slapped her hand on the table. "I think you both need to remember that I'm sitting right in front of you." She stabbed a French fry into the ketchup on her plate. "You're supposed to be taking my mind off things with this lunch." Her gaze narrowed on Galen. "I heard Mama call you this morning. Don't pretend you're here out of the goodness of your heart."

He shrugged but looked slightly guilty. "She's worried about you. We all are."

"I'm not the first girl to be hurt by a man." Delaney bit down on the fry. "Don't tell me you've never broken a girl's heart."

"I— You— Don't— This isn't about me," he stammered.

"Do you want to give Cisco another chance?" Stacey asked softly. "Do you still love him?"

"I don't know. He's called every day, left the sweetest

messages, sent flowers to the house each morning. But I don't know how I feel right now." She moved her food around on her plate, keeping her gaze averted from either of her siblings. Because she did know and if they looked her in the eye, they'd know, too. She loved Cisco now, maybe even more than she had before. Which made her quite possibly the biggest fool on the planet.

The fact that he'd kept the details of his work from her still stung, but now that the sharpness had dulled, she could begin to understand what had kept him from sharing everything. It was true, she wouldn't have trusted him and despite what she'd said, there was no way she would have agreed to help him when they'd first made their agreement. It was only getting to know him better, understanding that he was more than his big-city reputation, that had given Delaney enough faith in him to believe he wasn't out to make a fast deal.

She'd been able to look beyond his mask to see the man he was underneath his polished facade. She understood why that was important better than most. As much as she wanted to find a local cowboy to share her life with, no man before Cisco had seen her as an individual and not just the baby of the Fortune Jones family. But could she risk trusting him again?

A shiver ran up her back just as Stacey whispered, "Uh-oh."

Delaney didn't need to look up to know that Cisco had walked into the Grill. She did anyway, unable to stop herself. Their gazes met and her heart stammered at the pain in his eyes, at her body's reaction to him. She was at once hot and cold, struggling to remain seated and not go to him.

He took a step toward her, but she saw his father put a

hand on Cisco's shoulder, holding him back. At the same time, Galen pushed aside his plate and made to stand. "I can't believe he has the nerve to even look at you. I'm going to—"

"Do nothing," Delaney interrupted, grabbing her brother's wrist in her fingers before he could move away. "Leave him alone, Galen. Stacey's right. This is my choice."

"Then you do still love him?" Galen settled back in the booth reluctantly.

She glanced at Cisco again. He continued to stare at her until Orlando pulled him away, toward a table at the other side of the restaurant. Delaney swallowed. "I never stopped loving him, although I don't know if that's enough to make things better between us."

"If the way he looks at you is any indication," Stacey said, "his feelings are just as strong. People make mistakes." She gestured to their brother. "Men especially. Sometimes a second chance is a good thing."

"And sometimes," Galen answered, "you're just asking for more trouble."

Delaney closed her eyes for a moment, still not sure whether she agreed with her brother or sister.

Chapter Sixteen

"She's gone, so you can settle down a bit." Orlando watched Cisco over the brim of his coffee cup.

Cisco didn't need his father to tell him that Delaney had left the restaurant. It was as if the connection he felt for her had only grown stronger since they'd been apart. The energy in the room changed, deflated, when she left. The flash of pain to his heart at seeing her and being reminded of how he'd hurt her subsided once again to a blunt ache.

"She still won't take my calls," he muttered.

"Do you blame her?"

"How can I fix this if she won't talk to me? I need to make her understand why I did what I did."

"Maybe she understands more than you think." Orlando shrugged. "That could be part of the problem."

"What does that mean?"

His father waited to answer until the server had set down their food, but Cisco had no appetite. He hadn't been able to sleep, had barely been able to eat, since Delaney had sent him away from her sister's house.

"You're successful and driven, son. That's no secret. But a girl doesn't want to worry that you're going to put your career before her. So far you haven't given Delaney a reason to believe you'll do otherwise."

"Is it a bad thing to be successful? I've worked hard for my career, Dad. You did the same thing with the air force. I'm not trying to excuse the fact that I didn't tell Delaney everything when I should have. I was wrong, and I want to make it up to her."

Orlando shook his head. "Work isn't bad, but if you let the work consume you, there's so much you'll miss in life. You've always been focused on your goals, Cisco. But I have a feeling your priorities are changing, and I want to make sure you honor that. Yes, I had a good career, but your mother was always number one for me. Nothing was as important as her."

Cisco ran his hands through his hair, frustrated that there was no easy solution to this situation. "How did you know Mom was the one? What made it so different with her?"

"Who she was made it different," his father answered, leaning back in his chair, a wistful smile curving his mouth. "She was beautiful, of course, plus smart and funny. She was patient with me, too. Things weren't always easy between us, especially at the beginning. There were... Well, I'll just say that a love worth having is worth fighting for. Your mother made me a better person. Just being around her changed who I was on the inside. Do you understand what I'm talking about?"

Cisco didn't answer for several moments. He thought about his parents, how he'd known them only as a rock-solid partnership. Their love had been the foundation of the Mendoza family, and he never would have guessed they'd ever struggled to make it work. But now he saw them beyond the lens of his happy childhood. Their will-ingness to do the work it took to make their marriage last was what made their love so strong. If there was one thing Cisco had never shied away from, it was hard work.

He took a deep breath, the vise that had gripped his chest for the past several days slowly loosening. "I'm pretty sure I do, Dad. Thank you."

Orlando smiled and opened his mouth to speak, but Matteo grabbed the back of the empty seat and slid into it before he could. "Are we talking more about how roy-ally my perfect brother has messed up his perfect life?" he said, cuffing Cisco gently on the shoulder before pick-ing up the burger from Cisco's plate and taking a large bite. "Because I want in on that."

"Give it your best shot," Cisco answered, his mind already spinning as he tried to come up with a plan for how to win Delaney back once and for all. "I'm an idiot."

Matteo crumpled up his napkin and threw it on the table. "It kind of ruins the fun when you admit it."

"Ease up," Orlando said in his father-knows-best tone.

"I'm only joking," Matteo answered. "Believe it or not, I like having you around, even though you can be a smug, pompous jack—"

"Matteo," their father growled.

Cisco barked out a laugh. "He's right, Dad."

"I like you even better with Delaney." Matteo waved the waitress away when she came toward the table, then helped himself to a long drink of Cisco's iced tea. "She makes you almost human."

Cisco glanced at his father, who gave him an approving nod. "She won't speak to me or take my calls," he told his brother. "It makes it difficult to grovel."

"Don't give up," Orlando told him, his voice gentle and serious at the same time. "If you really love her, don't ever give up. Whatever it takes."

"Do you love her enough?" Matteo asked.

Cisco met his brother's dark eyes, so similar to his own, and nodded. "But I don't know how to make her believe me. I'm pretty sure her whole family hates me, which doesn't help matters. Hell, Gabi will barely speak to me."

"The Fortunes will come around," Matteo said, his certainty at odds with Cisco's worry. "They're a...complicated family. They've been through a lot and have overcome it. You have to make Delaney understand that you're in this for the right reasons and the long haul. I'd bet her family will support whatever she decides."

"Then I have to find a way to convince her," Cisco agreed. He pressed his palms on the worn table as an idea occurred to him. "And I think you and Rachel can help me. Can I count on you, bro?"

"A chance to bail *you* out of trouble for once?" Matteo picked up the burger again. "Count me in. Mendoza to the rescue."

Cisco felt adrenaline course through him. Not the kind he'd experienced as he worked a real estate deal. This was bigger, deeper, and he welcomed the intensity, let it soak into his bones. He wouldn't have ever guessed his life would end up on its current course, but nothing was going to stop him from getting what he wanted.

* * *

"This was a mistake," Delaney said on a moan, splashing water across her face in the restroom at the Hollows Cantina two nights later.

"You can't hide in here all night." Stacey handed her a paper towel, then leaned a hip against the granite counter. "The food is probably getting cold and the guys are going to wonder where we went."

"Weren't you the one who told me to give Cisco a second chance?" Delaney dried her cheeks and hands, turning to her sister. "I thought we were having a casual dinner, meeting Colton for Mexican and margaritas. I wanted you to take my mind off Cisco. Instead you've dragged me out on a double date."

"It's not exactly a double date," Stacey said patiently. "Jon is an old friend of Colton's and he's passing through town just for the night, so we invited him along with us."

"He brought me flowers." Delaney threw up her hands in frustration. "That feels an awful lot like a date."

Stacey looked a tiny bit abashed. "Colton mentioned to him that you just went through a tough breakup. He wanted to make you feel better."

"I want Cisco to make me feel better," Delaney answered, trying not to sound as desperate as she felt. After she'd seen him at the Grill, Cisco had stopped calling and texting her. Forty-eight full hours had gone by without a single word from him. Then this afternoon a package had arrived at the ranch. She'd opened the box to find a pair of the most perfect red cowboy boots made from soft, thick leather and exactly her size. There was no card included, but they were expensive, definitely custom-made, and she knew without a doubt that Cisco had sent them. She couldn't imagine how much he'd spent to have a pair of boots made and shipped so quickly, but what touched her was that in the midst of everything going on, he re- membered how upset she'd been about losing her favor- ite pair of boots when she'd hurt her ankle.

Her mother had been shocked when she'd burst into fat, drippy tears as she'd tried them on. Delaney had re- treated to her room, only to have Stacey appear an hour later, insisting on going out to dinner. It was clear Jeanne Marie had made the suggestion, so Delaney couldn't say no.

Now she was at the Cantina, with a very kind, hand- some stranger waiting at the table. She was wearing boots given to her by a man who confused and infuriated her even as he made her love him even more with his thought- ful gesture. Colton's friend Jon owned a ranch in south- west Oklahoma. He was clear-eyed and uncomplicated, just the sort of guy Delaney had always imagined herself settling down with. Until Cisco. The only man who made her feel things—want things—she hadn't even known existed in life.

"I'm not telling you to forget about Cisco and move on with Jon." Stacey smoothed a loose strand of hair away from Delaney's face. "But have fun tonight. If things are meant to be with Cisco, they will work themselves out. You hiding away at the ranch crying your eyes out all day isn't going to help."

"I haven't been crying all day." That part was true. There might be a hole in her heart, but working on a ranch didn't leave time for hours of self-reflection. She'd gone back to work, keeping busy so she wouldn't be tempted to sink into more melancholy. But the boots... Stacey couldn't possibly blame her for reacting to the boots.

Her sister leaned forward for a quick hug. "Come on,

Delaney. Let's go back to the table and have a nice dinner. Jon doesn't have expectations. Just enjoy tonight."

"I'll try." Delaney followed her sister through the restaurant, waving to Wendy Fortune Mendoza as she went.

"Thank you again for the flowers," she said to Jon when she got to the table. "It was really nice of you."

"My pleasure," the handsome cowboy told her. He gave her a friendly smile that just made her heart hurt more.

No expectations. Enjoy tonight, she reminded herself. He stood as she sat next to him, adjusting the small bouquet at the edge of the table. Her eyes tracked to the front of the restaurant and she was suddenly grateful for the chair underneath her. Her legs turned to rubber and she landed with a plop, her fingers still holding on to the flowers, lifting them as if they were a shield. Cisco had walked into the restaurant with Rachel Robinson.

Fresh pain washed over Delaney again. From everything Rachel had told her and Delaney had witnessed, her friend was deeply in love with Matteo Mendoza. Then why was she here with Cisco? Why was his hand on her back as Wendy walked them through the restaurant?

He glanced toward her table and she registered shock and something else on his face.

"The yellow ones match your hair," a voice whispered near her ear.

She turned to Jon, who smiled at her, unaware of the scene playing out in the restaurant. Delaney forced a smile, glancing over her shoulder to see Cisco scowling in her direction.

"Oh, no," Stacey muttered, her eyes following Delaney's. "This could be a problem."

"No trouble tonight," Delaney said, turning back to

the table and swallowing down tears. "Maybe I needed to see that, Stacey. It just proves I should be out having fun." She smiled again, surprised when her cheeks didn't crack from the effort. She felt wooden and empty, but she wasn't going to let Cisco see that. Obviously it hadn't taken him long to bounce back. It still shocked her to see him with Rachel, and she wondered if Matteo knew about this dinner. The cowboy boots were suddenly heavy on her feet, a fresh reminder of how naive she was. Part of her wanted to take them off and hurl the boots at Cisco's handsome head.

But Delaney wouldn't give him the satisfaction of knowing how much seeing him with Rachel affected her. Instead she straightened her spine, gritted her teeth and proceeded to laugh and flirt with the man next to her, even as fresh heartbreak threatened to drown her in misery.

Chapter Seventeen

"You should go over there and explain that this isn't how it looks," Rachel told Cisco for the third time since they'd been seated in the Cantina.

"And interrupt her date?" Cisco shook his head, his jaw so tight it ached. "No way."

"She probably thinks *we're* on a date," Rachel argued.

"That's ridiculous. You're with Matteo—"

"Who's running late." Rachel moved in her seat, looking toward the front of the restaurant. "I wish he would just get here already."

"I'm not going to make a scene and if I tried to talk to Delancy with that cowboy hanging all over her, there would definitely be a scene."

"It doesn't seem like he's hanging on her," Rachel told him, shifting her gaze. "They are sitting next to each other. No touching."

"She has flowers," Cisco bit out. "And stop staring."

Rachel ignored him. "She's also wearing the cowboy boots you described. That's a good sign."

"Not as good as if she were having dinner with me instead of him."

"You said yourself you need to earn a place in her life." Rachel flipped open her menu. "Isn't that what this night's about? Are you having second thoughts? Because love in real life isn't easy, Cisco. You'll have to stick by her side whether things are good or bad. Delaney is a bit of a firecracker…"

"I love that about her," he said, and didn't bother to hide the emotion in his voice. He trusted Rachel.

"Then you'll have to fight for her no matter what. Even when it would be easier to walk away."

"I plan to," he agreed.

"And no more secrets," Rachel continued. "For love to work, you have to be willing to lay it all on the line. I know it isn't easy—trust me."

He saw a shadow cross her eyes and wondered for a moment what put it there. He was certain it wasn't his brother, who was so madly in love he could barely see straight. "I'm glad things worked out with you and Matteo. You make him happy, Rachel."

She grinned and he was happy to see it reached her eyes. "It goes both ways. I hope you can find that same happiness with Delaney."

"Me, too." A waitress approached the table and Cisco ordered a beer and Rachel a margarita plus nachos to share. They'd wait for the rest of their group before getting food. As he looked up, he saw Delaney, Stacey, Colton and the cowboy walking toward the front entrance. Delaney kept her gaze straight ahead, but Stacey turned and gave him a small wave and apologetic smile. For some reason that gesture made him feel a little better.

He knew it didn't truly matter who Delaney was out with tonight. There could be a mile-long line of cowboys in front of her door and he'd fight his way through all of them to get to her. As far as Cisco was concerned, Delaney was his. He just needed to prove it to her in a way she couldn't ignore.

Matteo and Christopher Fortune walked into the Cantina a few minutes later, both looking a little dazed.

"You ran into Stacey and Delaney, I take it," Rachel said with a laugh as Matteo took the seat next to her and leaned in for a kiss.

Matteo nodded, swallowing visibly. "I thought Gabi was scary when she was mad, but those two…"

"My sisters are a force to be reckoned with," Christopher said, "especially when they're together. It's probably good that Kinsley had another meeting tonight she couldn't cancel. She'd love the chance to tell you what she thinks of how you've handled this." He turned to Cisco as he sank into the last empty chair at the table. "You've got to make things better with Delaney, man. You picked the wrong cowgirl to cross."

"I'm trying," Cisco said for what felt like the tenth time in the past few days. "She's not making it easy."

"Things that are worth having aren't always easy," Christopher told him, and ordered a beer when the waitress came back to the table. He took one of the cheese-covered chips from the plate of nachos she set in front of them.

"That's why I wanted to talk to you." Cisco scrubbed his hand across his face, trying to settle his emotions. He had one shot with Christopher Fortune and he didn't want to mess this up, too. "I appreciate you meeting me here. I know I'm not the most popular man in the Fortune Jones family right now."

"Understatement," Christopher said with a short laugh. "I like it. You're lucky I think so highly of Rachel and your brother. They've assured me you're not quite the rat bastard everyone around here assumes."

"Great," Cisco muttered. Then he took a deep breath. He wasn't going to give up on Delaney and his chance with her. It was scary and harder than the most complicated deal he'd ever brokered. But she was worth every change he was making in his life. She was the *reason* for every change.

"So you're working with Alden Moore?" Christopher asked, unknowingly giving Cisco the perfect way to broach the subject that had made him set up this meeting in the first place.

He glanced at Matteo, who gave him an encouraging nod. Funny, that. He'd always been the one to lead and push his siblings. Surprisingly, it felt good to rely on his family's support after so long on his own.

"Not anymore," he answered, meeting Christopher's gaze. "We couldn't come to an agreement about the plans for the condo development, so I resigned from Cowboy Country earlier today."

Christopher's brows rose. "Is that so? I did a little digging on you, Mendoza. From what I heard, Moore Entertainment had big plans for you on their executive team."

"I don't care about their plans." Cisco tipped back his beer bottle, taking a long swallow. "I still hope Cowboy Country succeeds. If they change focus and incorporate some of the things that make Horseback Hollow special into the theme park, it could be good for the town. But I won't be involved going forward."

"Where does that leave you?" Christopher bit into another chip. "Are you heading back to Miami? Because Delaney—"

"I'm not going back to Florida," Cisco interrupted. "I'm staying in Horseback Hollow. My future is here, with Delaney if I can convince her of that. You might have heard I was investing a decent chunk of my own money in the Cowboy Country venture. That's not going to happen at this point. I want a clean break with Moore Entertainment." He shifted in his seat so he more fully faced Christopher. "I want to make a donation—a significant donation—to the local branch of the Fortune Foundation."

He wasn't looking for a ticker-tape parade at the announcement, but he also hadn't expected the way Christopher's eyes narrowed on him.

"It's true," Rachel said quickly, filling the awkward silence. "I've told Cisco about the foundation's plans for the community and he wants to be a part of that. He's committed to Horseback Hollow."

"Or he's trying to buy his way into the family," Christopher offered. His tone held no temper, but it was clear he doubted Cisco's motivations.

Things worth having aren't always easy, Cisco repeated in his head. "I understand why you might think that," he answered, still holding Christopher's gaze. "I haven't given you a reason not to, but I'm doing this because I believe in the work you have planned here. The time I spent on your family's ranch meant a lot to me, and not just because of Delaney. There are strong values in that way of life, deep traditions and roots. I'd never experienced anything like it."

"So you're turning into an overnight cowboy?"

Cisco shook his head. "I wouldn't go that far. I respect your father, but not everyone is cut out for ranching."

"Amen to that," Christopher muttered.

"This place is special," Cisco continued. "My family might have seen that before I did…"

"He was always slow on the uptake," Matteo offered.

Christopher flashed a grin. "You two remind me of my brothers."

Cisco figured that was a good start since Christopher said it with a smile. "Even if Delaney won't take me back, that doesn't change my decision about giving the money to the foundation. I want to make a contribution to this town. Give me a chance to do that?"

"What will you do if she won't have you again? What happens then?"

"I keep fighting for her," Cisco answered without hesitation. "For as long as it takes."

"That's what I wanted to hear." Christopher clinked his beer bottle against Cisco's. "Delaney deserves a man who won't give up on her."

"I'm that man, Christopher. That much I promise."

The sky was vast and robin's-egg blue as Cisco turned down the long driveway that led to the Fortune Jones ranch the next afternoon. The days were becoming increasingly warmer as they got closer to Memorial Day and the unofficial start of summer. The holiday weekend would also mark the planned opening of the Cowboy Country theme park, but Cisco didn't miss being a part of the planning and preparations. A bead of sweat trickled down his neck under his shirt collar, less a result of the heat than his nerves.

Christopher had agreed to call his parents and set up a time for Cisco to come to the ranch. Without that, Cisco was pretty sure Deke Jones would have met him at the door with a shotgun in hand. He knew how Orlando would have felt about a man who dared to hurt Gabi.

He pulled around the house and parked in front of the barn. Climbing out of the truck, he glanced back at the ranch house. Curtains fluttered in one of the upper windows. Delaney.

The thought that the conversation he was about to have might be the final hurtle before he could see her again spurred him on. Deke was standing to one side of the corral closest to the barn. It looked as if he was working on a section of fence along with one of the ranch hands. Cisco wiped his palms on his crisp jeans and moved forward.

Deke straightened as Cisco approached and said something to the younger man, who glanced at Cisco, then headed for the far side of the corral.

"Mr. Jones," Cisco said when he got closer. "Thank you for agreeing to talk to me today. I know I'm not—"

"Might as well call me Deke and don't thank me yet," the weathered rancher answered, adjusting his hat as he spoke. "My girl's been crying a fair bit in the last couple of days and you seem to be the reason." He kept his tone soft, but that gravelly voice was pure steel underneath.

"I'm sorry," Cisco began, but Deke lifted his hand.

"Not me who needs to hear that apology, son."

"You can bet I'll be making up for how I handled things with Delaney for a long time."

One side of the cowboy's mouth twitched. "If Delaney has any say in it, you certainly will."

"It will be my great honor," Cisco told Deke. "And that's why I wanted to talk to you before I go see Delaney. I hope to love and honor your daughter for a very long time. I have a great deal of respect for you and your family, the life you've built."

"I sure as hell hope you don't plan to hug me at the end of this speech."

"No, sir." Cisco shifted, toed the ground with one boot, then wiped his hands on his jeans again. His throat was dry and scratchy. He wished he had a glass of water, or better yet, whiskey. He'd never relied on liquid courage, but he could sure use some now. Instead he cleared his throat. Deke Fortune Jones was an old-fashioned man's man. Cisco had a feeling Delaney's father wouldn't countenance any weakness in a man who came courting his youngest child. "I love your daughter, sir. I want to ask her to marry me and I'd like your permission before I speak with her."

Deke didn't answer, only lifted one thick brow.

Cisco wanted to rush on with a stream of reasons why he deserved Delaney's hand even after he'd hurt her so badly. But he remained as still and silent as Deke. The man would make up his own mind, no matter how much Cisco pleaded his case. He knew Delaney would never be his if her family disapproved. They were a part of who she was as much as this town, and he would never ask her to give them up. So he didn't say anything more, just stood stock-still, waiting for his fate to be decided.

Delaney had been pacing back and forth in her bedroom for the past thirty minutes, stealing glances out the window and wondering where Cisco had gone.

He'd parked in front of the barn, but she'd still expected him to come to the house and it had taken every ounce of willpower she possessed not to run down the stairs to greet him. But he hadn't, at least not yet. Her father would be out in the corral, although how Cisco could manage a half-hour conversation with her dad she had no idea. She sank down to the carpet in front of her dresser and drew her knees up to her chest, using one finger to trace the flower inlay on the boots Cisco had made for her. She forced herself to stay there instead of standing watch at the window. If Cisco wanted to talk, he knew where to find her. If not, then she—

"Delaney." Her mother's muffled call came from the bottom of the staircase. "You have a visitor, sweetie."

Panic drove Delaney to her feet in an instant. Panic that Cisco had come to fight for her and she wouldn't be able to resist him. Panic that he'd come to tell her she wasn't worth the effort and she'd lost her chance to be his.

She glanced in the mirror, not surprised that she looked pale and tired. She finger-combed her hair and pinched her cheeks for color, then walked down the hallway to the stairs before she chickened out.

Cisco waited at the bottom, along with her mother. His dark chocolate eyes were intense yet unreadable as he watched her.

"You two head to the den for some privacy," her mother said, giving Delaney's arm a reassuring squeeze. "I'm going to make fresh lemonade, so if you get thirsty, just holler."

She turned to Cisco, leaning forward to give him a maternal kiss on the cheek. "It's good to see you again, Cisco."

Delaney's heart stuttered. How pathetic that she was

reduced to being jealous of her mother and her easy af-fectionate nature with people.

"Thank you, ma'am," Cisco answered, turning his gaze to Jeanne Marie. "I'm sorry for all the turmoil I've caused around here."

Her mother's smile was gentle. "When you've raised seven children, trouble and turmoil are part of life." She headed to the kitchen as Delaney led Cisco into the cozy den.

She marched to the edge of the room in front of the fireplace, expecting that he'd take a seat on the well-worn sofa. But when she turned, he was standing right behind her. So close that the scent of bergamot and spice sur-rounded her. So close that she could see faint lines of fa-tigue bracketing his eyes and mouth. He wore a crisp blue button-down shirt that made his skin look more golden than normal and dark Cinch jeans with cowboy boots, a style that was a mix of his city background and the weeks he'd spent in Horseback Hollow. It suited him and Del-aney realized he now seemed comfortable in both worlds.

It was hard to concentrate on anything beyond her body's reaction to him when he was this close. Her heart pounded, her stomach rolled and a tremble slipped through her as he gave her a tentative smile.

"Hello, Delaney," he said, his voice a low caress. He didn't move to touch her but still managed to invade every inch of her personal space.

"Can you back away a little?" she asked, her voice breathless. "I can't think when you're looming over me."

He stuffed his hands in his front pockets and rocked back on his boot heels. "Am I looming?"

"Definitely looming," she confirmed.

He took two large steps toward the couch. "Is this better?"

She nodded, then sucked her bottom lip between her teeth. It wasn't actually any better, because she only wanted to sway closer to him. She forced herself to remain still.

"What can I do for you, Cisco?" There, that sounded formal and indifferent, as if she had better ways to be spending this late-spring afternoon.

"I'm sorry if you thought I was out with Rachel last night," he said quickly.

That wasn't what she'd expected. Cisco wasn't the type of guy to apologize for a simple misunderstanding, but it touched her that he was now. It was difficult to keep her feelings walled off from him when he was clearly going so far out of his comfort zone to make things right.

"Matteo was running late but he got to the restaurant shortly after you left. I would have told you, but you were… I didn't want to ruin your evening." He shrugged and suddenly looked uncertain.

Another piece of her heart's armor fell to the floor.

"It wasn't a date."

"He brought you flowers."

"Yes, but it wasn't a date."

He looked as if he wanted to argue but gave a short nod. "Thank you for telling me."

Oh, how Delaney hated and loved this at the same time. Loved how careful he was being with her but hated how that decorum was like a barrier between them. She'd never had much use for formality.

"Is that what you came to tell me?" She held her breath as he seemed to mull over his response.

"I quit my job at Cowboy Country," he answered after

a moment. "I told you Alden Moore would probably fire me, but I didn't wait for that to happen. I turned in my resignation letter yesterday morning."

Delaney tried to process what that meant but hadn't quite wrapped her mind around it when he continued, "I've donated the money I planned to invest in the condos to the Fortune Foundation."

"To Christopher? Is that why he was with Matteo at the restaurant?"

Cisco nodded again. "I want the money to be used to support the Horseback Hollow community."

"You bribed my brother?" Delaney blurted, disbelief hurtling through her. "And he went for it?"

Cisco took his balled hands out of his pockets, pressed them hard against his eyes, then jammed them back down again. "It's not a bribe," he said slowly. His voice held a weary edge. "Although that was his first suggestion, too. That's why Rachel facilitated the meeting. Christopher seemed even less inclined than you to return my calls."

"My family is a loyal bunch." Delaney wrapped her arms around her waist, unsure where this conversation was heading.

"I respect that. Christopher and I had a long talk last night. We're actually a lot alike. Both of us used to think the bottom line was all that mattered. That our success and all the trappings that went along with it were what made us who we were. Your brother changed when he met Kinsley…"

"She's been good for him," Delaney agreed.

"…and I changed when I met you," Cisco continued. "I changed because of you. I don't want to buy my way into your family. I needed to show you that my intentions, my heart, are in the right place. With you."

The air whooshed out her lungs as he spoke the words. They were exactly what she wanted to hear, but now that he'd said them, doubts bubbled to the surface again. "What if you only think you changed? What if I'm the latest deal you have to close? The rush is going to end eventually, Cisco. This connection—" she gestured between the two of them "—is bound to fade."

"Or grow deeper," he countered.

She bit her lip again to keep from crying. "I'm afraid to trust you," she told him on a shaky breath. As much as she liked to play tough, Delaney had to be honest with him. "I don't want to be a challenge to you now, then wake up a few weeks or months or years down the road to find you've gone off on your next adventure. I'm a simple cowgirl, Cisco. I told you that from the beginning. I like who I am. I love my life. I want you to be a part of it, but what if it doesn't last?"

"What if it lasts a lifetime?" He took a small velvet box from his pocket, holding it out in a hand that trembled slightly. "I love you, Delaney. I think I started to love you the moment I first saw you."

"At the barbecue," she whispered, unable to take her eyes off the box.

"At Gabi and Jude's wedding," Cisco clarified. "But I had no idea how important you'd become to me. You are a part of me, the best part of me. Hell, it took having a woman boss me around all over this ranch to make me realize what it takes to be a real man."

"I'm kind of a big deal on the ranch," she said with a small laugh.

"You're a big deal to me every minute of every day."

She continued to stare at the ring box until Cisco cleared his throat. She glanced up at him, unable to produce a sound as she looked into those dark eyes filled with so much love. For her.

As she watched, his gaze shuttered and he looked as though he was about to bolt. His fingers curled around the box as if he might shove it back into his pocket. She didn't understand and opened her mouth but still no words came. He closed his eyes for a moment, then opened them again, his eyes intense on her. "I know how much I hurt you, and I probably don't deserve a second chance. But I won't give up on you, Delaney. Your father told me the decision is yours and that's true—"

"You talked to my dad?" She felt her mouth drop open. It took some nerve to approach Deke Jones on a good day, let alone with the situation Cisco had caused clouding the water.

Cisco nodded. "I'll wait for you for as long as it takes. Every single damn day for the rest of my life, I'm going to wake up ready to prove that I can be—that I am—the man you deserve. Even if it takes forever."

Delaney snapped shut her mouth and licked her too-dry lips. Hope began to fizz through her, and she felt lit up like a sparkler on a summer night. "Was there something you wanted to ask me, Cisco?" He looked at her blankly and she raised one eyebrow. "I mean, that's a mighty-fine box you've got there but—"

Before she could finish the sentence, he'd dropped to one knee in front of her. He opened the box to reveal a perfect round center-cut diamond surrounded by tiny bezel-set chips. The ring glinted as the afternoon light caught it and her heart seemed to stop for an instant. It was perfect. He was perfect. "Delaney Fortune Jones, I love you more than I ever thought possible. Would you do me the very great honor of becoming my wife?"

He didn't look confident or cocky as he said the words, just full of love, hope and yearning. Delaney thought he'd never been more handsome.

"Yes," she whispered, and he rose to slip the ring onto her left hand, then gathered her in his arms, holding on so tight she thought he might never let go. She hoped he'd never let go.

"You will always know that you're my first priority," he said into her hair, peppering her with soft kisses as he spoke. "You are everything to me, Delaney. I love you."

"I love you, too," she said, tipping back her head to look into his eyes. "We're going to have the best life together."

He grinned at that. "The best ever," he agreed.

She gave him a saucy wink. "We should probably start with finding you a new job."

He shook his head. "The job will come," he told her. "We should definitely start with this…" Then he kissed her and she both lost and found herself as they explored each other. There was no doubt that Cisco Mendoza was hers for life. And she couldn't be happier.

* * * * *

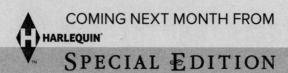

COMING NEXT MONTH FROM

HARLEQUIN®

SPECIAL EDITION

Available April 21, 2015

#2401 NOT QUITE MARRIED
The Bravos of Justice Creek • by Christine Rimmer
After a fling with Dalton Ames on an idyllic island, Clara Bravo wound up pregnant. She never told Dalton the truth, since the recently divorced hunk insisted he wasn't interested in a relationship. But when Dalton discovers Clara's secret, he's determined to create a forever-after with the Bravo beauty and their baby...no matter how much she protests!

#2402 MY FAIR FORTUNE
The Fortunes of Texas: Cowboy Country
by Nancy Robards Thompson
On the outside, PR guru Brodie Fortune Hayes is the perfect British gentleman. But on the inside, he's not as polished as he seems. When Brodie is hired to fix up the image of Horseback Hollow's Cowboy Country theme park, one lovely Texan—his former fling Caitlyn Moore—might just be the woman who can open his heart after all!

#2403 A FOREVER KIND OF FAMILY
Those Engaging Garretts! • by Brenda Harlen
Daddy. That's one role Ryan Garrett never thought he'd occupy...until his friend's death left him with custody of a fourteen-month-old. He definitely didn't count on gorgeous Harper Ross stepping in to help with little Oliver. As they butt heads and sparks fly, another Garrett bachelor finds the love of a lifetime!

#2404 FOLLOWING DOCTOR'S ORDERS
Texas Rescue • by Caro Carson
Dr. Brooke Brown has devoted her entire life to her career—but that doesn't mean she isn't susceptible to playboy firefighter Zach Bishop's smoldering good looks. A fling soon turns into so much more, but Brooke's tragic past and Zach's newly discovered future might stand in the way of the family they've always wanted.

#2405 FROM BEST FRIEND TO BRIDE
The St. Johns of Stonerock • by Jules Bennett
Police chief Cameron St. John has always loved his best friend, Megan Richards—and not just in a platonic way. But there's too much baggage for friendship to turn into romance, so Cameron sets his feelings aside...until Megan's life is threatened by her dangerous brother. Then Cameron will stop at nothing to protect her—and ensure their future together.

#2406 HIS PREGNANT TEXAS SWEETHEART
Peach Leaf, Texas • by Amy Woods
Katie Bloom has fallen on hard times. She's pregnant and alone, and the museum where she works is going out of business. Now Ryan Ford, the one who got away, walks into a local eatery, tempting her with his soulful good looks. Ryan's got secrets, but can he put Katie and her child above everything else to create a lifelong love?

REQUEST YOUR FREE BOOKS!

2 FREE NOVELS PLUS 2 FREE GIFTS!

⊕ HARLEQUIN®

SPECIAL EDITION

Life, Love & Family

YES! Please send me 2 FREE Harlequin® Special Edition novels and my 2 FREE gifts (gifts are worth about $10). After receiving them, if I don't wish to receive any more books, I can return the shipping statement marked "cancel." If I don't cancel, I will receive 6 brand-new novels every month and be billed just $4.74 per book in the U.S. or $5.24 per book in Canada. That's a savings of at least 14% off the cover price! It's quite a bargain! Shipping and handling is just 50¢ per book in the U.S. and 75¢ per book in Canada.* I understand that accepting the 2 free books and gifts places me under no obligation to buy anything. I can always return a shipment and cancel at any time. Even if I never buy another book, the two free books and gifts are mine to keep forever.

235/335 HDN F45Y

Name   (PLEASE PRINT)

Address   Apt. #

City   State/Prov.   Zip/Postal Code

Signature (if under 18, a parent or guardian must sign)

Mail to the **Harlequin® Reader Service:**
IN U.S.A.: P.O. Box 1867, Buffalo, NY 14240-1867
IN CANADA: P.O. Box 609, Fort Erie, Ontario L2A 5X3

Want to try two free books from another line?
Call 1-800-873-8635 or visit www.ReaderService.com.

* Terms and prices subject to change without notice. Prices do not include applicable taxes. Sales tax applicable in N.Y. Canadian residents will be charged applicable taxes. Offer not valid in Quebec. This offer is limited to one order per household. Not valid for current subscribers to Harlequin Special Edition books. All orders subject to credit approval. Credit or debit balances in a customer's account(s) may be offset by any other outstanding balance owed by or to the customer. Please allow 4 to 6 weeks for delivery. Offer available while quantities last.

Your Privacy—The Harlequin® Reader Service is committed to protecting your privacy. Our Privacy Policy is available online at www.ReaderService.com or upon request from the Harlequin Reader Service.

We make a portion of our mailing list available to reputable third parties that offer products we believe may interest you. If you prefer that we not exchange your name with third parties, or if you wish to clarify or modify your communication preferences, please visit us at www.ReaderService.com/consumerschoice or write to us at Harlequin Reader Service Preference Service, P.O. Box 9062, Buffalo, NY 14269. Include your complete name and address.

HSE13R

SPECIAL EXCERPT FROM

HARLEQUIN®

SPECIAL EDITION

Harper Ross and Ryan Garrett are joint guardians for their best friends' baby...but the heat between them is undeniable. Can passion turn to love...and create the family they both long for?

Read on for a sneak preview of
A FOREVER KIND OF FAMILY,
the latest installment in **Brenda Harlen**'s
THOSE ENGAGING GARRETTS! *miniseries.*

When Harper had gone back to work a few days after the funeral, Ryan had offered to be the one to get up in the night with Oliver so that she could sleep through. It wasn't his fault that she heard every sound that emanated from Oliver's room, across the hall from her own.

Thankfully, she worked behind the scenes at *Coffee Time with Caroline*, Charisma's most popular morning news show, so the dark circles under her eyes weren't as much a problem as the fog that seemed to have enveloped her brain. And that fog was definitely a problem.

"Do you want me to get him a drink?" she asked as Ryan zipped up Oliver's sleeper.

"I can manage," he assured her. "Go get some sleep."

Just as she decided that she would, Oliver—now clean and dry—stretched his arms out toward her. "Up."

Ryan deftly scooped him up in one arm. "I've got you, buddy."

The little boy shook his head, reaching for Harper.

"Up."

"Harper has to go night-night, just like you," Ryan said.

"Up," Oliver insisted.

Ryan looked at her questioningly.

She shrugged. "I've got breasts."

She'd spoken automatically, her brain apparently stuck somewhere between asleep and awake, without regard to whom she was addressing or how he might respond.

Of course, his response was predictably male—his gaze dropped to her chest and his lips curved in a slow and sexy smile. "Yeah—I'm aware of that."

Her cheeks burned as her traitorous nipples tightened beneath the thin cotton of her ribbed tank top in response to his perusal, practically begging for his attention. She lifted her arms to reach for the baby, and to cover up her breasts. "I only meant that he prefers a softer chest to snuggle against."

"Can't blame him for that," Ryan agreed, transferring the little boy to her.

Oliver immediately dropped his head onto her shoulder and dipped a hand down the front of her top to rest on the slope of her breast.

"The kid's got some slick moves," Ryan noted.

Harper felt her cheeks burning again as she moved over to the chair and settled in to rock the baby.

Fall in love with A FOREVER KIND OF FAMILY by Brenda Harlen, available May 2015 wherever Harlequin® Special Edition books and ebooks are sold.

www.Harlequin.com

HSEEXP0415

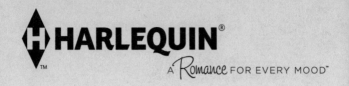

HARLEQUIN®
A *Romance* FOR EVERY MOOD™

Love the Harlequin book you just read?

Your opinion matters.

Review this book on your favorite book site, review site, blog or your own social media properties and share your opinion with other readers!

Be sure to connect with us at:
Harlequin.com/Newsletters
Facebook.com/HarlequinBooks
Twitter.com/HarlequinBooks

JUST CAN'T GET ENOUGH?

Join our social communities
and talk to us online.

You will have access to the latest
news on upcoming titles and special
promotions, but most importantly,
you can talk to other fans about your
favorite Harlequin reads.

Harlequin.com/Community

Facebook.com/HarlequinBooks

Twitter.com/HarlequinBooks

Pinterest.com/HarlequinBooks

THE WORLD IS BETTER WITH

Romance

Harlequin has everything from contemporary, passionate and heartwarming to suspenseful and inspirational stories.

Whatever your mood,
we have a romance just for you!

Connect with us to find your next great read, special offers and more.

f /HarlequinBooks

🐦 @HarlequinBooks

www.HarlequinBlog.com

www.Harlequin.com/Newsletters

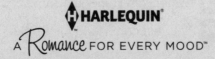

H HARLEQUIN®

A *Romance* FOR EVERY MOOD™

www.Harlequin.com